MEMOIR OF THE LATE GEORGE WASHINGTON,

By an Associate.

MEMOIR

OF THE LATE

George Washington,

By an Associate.

Let us now praise famous men, and our fathers that begat us.

——Ecclesiasticus 44:1.

H. ALBERTUS BOLI

PITTSBURGH:

Dr. Boli's Celebrated Publishing Empire, 2020

MEMOIR OF THE LATE
GEORGE WASHINGTON,

By an Associate.

CHAPTER I.

*My meeting with Washington.—Expedition to oust the
French.—French will not be ousted.—Washington's
dispatch, and its reception.*

Of Washington's childhood I have nothing to say. The
tale has been told well enough by one who, if he was
not better informed than I, has at least been more
imaginative. I first encountered Washington as a
young man in need of a boat.

When the knock came at my door, I was, I admit,
rather surprised, and not a little apprehensive. Visitors came seldom to my cabin on the Potomac, far
upstream as it was and at the very edge of English settlement; and it was not out of the question that I

might find some lawless savage waiting for me outside the door, ready to take my scalp to add to his personal museum. With that possibility in mind, I seized my staff, which I have always found more useful at close quarters than a musket or a rifle, and opened the door with a quick jerk.

I saw no one before me until I heard a voice saying, "Pardon the intrusion"; then I looked down and beheld a small man, about four feet nine inches tall, looking up at me. He was dressed in military fashion in buff and blue, and he was holding an empty burlap sack. He seemed barely more than a boy, but there was something commanding in his bearing, and a sort of inherent dignity in his address, that compelled my immediate respect.

"Pardon the intrusion," said he, "but I have urgent need of a boat, and I was hoping I might perhaps make use of yours."

"You need to cross the river?" I asked.

"Yes, to retrieve the money that was in this bag." He held up the empty sack. "There were fifty-six Spanish milled dollars in here."

"But how did they get across the river?"

"Well, I—" He looked down at the ground. "I'm afraid I threw them."

I fear I may have responded with undignified incredulity. "You *threw* them?"

"In a moment of absence of mind," he replied, looking up at me again. "You see, as a boy I whiled away so many hours throwing dollars across the Rappahannock that the thing became an ingrained habit, as it were. When there is a river, and there are dollars, they always seem to end up on the other side."

"That does seem inconvenient," I said.

"But there is, I believe, a wise saying that applies very well to such inconveniences." From his breast pocket he produced a small, well-thumbed copybook, and he leafed through it until he found the page he desired. "'When in good company at dinner, do not pick your teeth until after the ladies have withdrawn.'" He closed the book and returned it to his pocket.

"Well," I said, "I am at your service, Mr..."

"Oh! Washington, sir. George Washington, adjutant to Governor Dunwoodie, sir."

"Dinwiddie?"

"Yes, sir. Forgive me—I ought to have introduced myself at once. I'm on an important mission from the governor, sir, and the cares of my commission must have been weighing heavily on my mind."

I extended my hand, and the little man gripped it with surprising firmness. "Christopher Gist, sir," I said, "and my boat is at your service. I shall be happy to take you across."

"There are several of us in the party," Washington said. "Allow me to introduce you." He turned aside to let me through the door, and I stepped out into the cold November air. Four other men were waiting out there, and Washington introduced them one by one.

"This is Mr. Gadelle, an Indian trader recommended to me as familiar with the ways of the savages."

"Yup," said Mr. Gadelle.

"And this is Mr. Beadle, another Indian trader, whom I have persuaded to accompany me to consult on the commercial possibilities of certain lands I possess near the Forks of the Ohio."

"Yup," said Mr. Beadle.

"Mr. Beadle and Mr. Gadelle are from Connecticut," Washington explained. "And this is Mr. Von
Schloss."

"Guten Tag, mein Herr," said Mr. Von Schloss.

"As my mission is to confront the French and warn
them to depart the Ohio country, I have engaged Mr.
Von Schloss as an interpreter," Washington explained.
"And this is Parson Weems."

"How do you do, sir?" said the ecclesiastical gentleman.

"Parson Weems will use his most persuasive
rhetoric to redeem the French officers from the
wickedness of popery," said Washington. "When that
is accomplished, they will doubtless become much
more friendly toward us, their fellow Christians."

"It is an honor to make your acquaintance, gentlemen," said I. "I fear it may take more than one crossing to transport all of you and your baggage across the
river, but I can—"

"Oh, that will not be necessary," said Washington.
"It will suffice to transport me so that I may retrieve
the dollars, and then you can bring me back, and we
shall be on our way."

"But aren't you headed for the Ohio country?"

"Yes, that is our destination."

"Then you'll have to cross the river. North is *that*
way."

"Is it?" He looked puzzled for a moment, and then
seemed to reach a sudden decision. "Mr. Gist, you
seem to be extraordinarily well informed in matters of
geography. Would you consider serving the great

country of Virginia in the capacity of a scout or guide? I have sore need of a man with your obvious gifts."

I did not accept his invitation at first. But when he pressed it on me a second and third time, I reconsidered. I had no wife or children, nor even so much as a hunting dog, to tie me to my simple cabin. If I could be of service to Virginia, ought I not to place my meager abilities at her command? After some hesitation, I accepted the proposal.

"Governor Denwaddie and I will be most grateful," said Washington. "And now, if you will conduct us to the other side, we can be on our way."

"It might be best to set off tomorrow," I suggested. "The day is already far advanced, and I have some small preparations to make before I leave. You gentlemen are welcome to my cabin tonight, where, poor though it may be, you will at least be warm and comfortable. Tomorrow we may start at dawn, and we should be able to make good progress on the Indian trail."

"A fine suggestion," Washington agreed. "Only—"

He hesitated, looked to the left and the right, and lowered his voice.

"You haven't heard a sound around here that might be described as 'braying,' have you?"

I listened. Except for the usual sounds—the river, the wind in the trees, and a crow in the cherry tree near the riverbank—I heard nothing, and certainly nothing that could have been called braying.

"I don't think so," I answered.

"One can never be too careful," said Washington. "Now, if you would be so kind as to take me across to pick up my dollars, I shall be most grateful to you."

"By all means. Please follow me."

"Just a moment." He turned to Mr. Von Schloss and pointed to another burlap sack, this one sitting on the ground and obviously full. "I rely on you, Mr. Von Schloss, to guard that bag. It is of the highest importance."

"Guten Tag, mein Herr," said Mr. Von Schloss.

"Well done. And now, Mr. Gist, to the boat."

We walked down to the riverbank, and had almost reached my little rowboat, when suddenly Washington came to an abrupt halt.

"Is that a cherry tree?" he asked so quietly that at first I could not hear him distinctly.

"I beg your pardon?"

"It *is* a cherry tree, isn't it?"

I looked down at the man, and in just a few seconds, there in the November chill, large beads of perspiration had formed on his forehead.

"Yes," I answered cautiously. "A wild black cherry. Very productive of fruit in its season."

Washington was trembling all over. "Hatchet," he whispered through gritted teeth. And then he shook his head vigorously. "Please forgive me, Mr. Gist. I am in perfect control of my actions." His manner, however, suggested the opposite, and I wondered whether he was speaking more to convince himself than to inform me.

We made the crossing with no difficulty, as the river was calm at the time, and on the opposite shore we easily found the dollars we were seeking. They were distributed over a remarkably small area. "You must have very good aim with a dollar," I remarked.

"It is not boasting to say that I can throw a dollar farther than anyone else in the colonies, and with greater accuracy." He picked up one of the dollars, and, turning to face the river, suddenly launched it with almost incredible force. It sailed through the air until I lost sight of it; and then, a few moments later, we heard a sharp yelp from the opposite shore.

"Oh, dear," said Washington, gazing in that direction. Then he turned away. "Well, it can't be helped now. As they say..." He pulled the copybook out of his pocket and thumbed through it rapidly until he found his page. "A pair of clean stockings every day will do much to improve one's standing among men of discernment." Then he replaced the book in his pocket and resumed filling his sack with dollars.

When we returned with the sack of fifty-five dollars, we found Mr. Gadelle prone on the ground. Washington passed the cherry tree as quickly as he could and then addressed Mr. Beadle apologetically. "I appear to have struck Mr. Gadelle with a Spanish milled dollar."

"Yup," replied Mr. Beadle.

"He'll come around soon enough," Parson Weems remarked. "They generally do."

"Under the circumstances," said Washington, "I think I ought to let him keep the dollar as usual."

"Yup," replied Mr. Beadle.

And indeed Mr. Gadelle recovered soon afterward and took possession of the dollar without further remark.

I managed to feed the five guests and myself fairly well, and when we retired, though the cabin was small, we slept soundly, except for a brief moment when Washington shouted the name "Irving" in his sleep, waking the rest of us but not himself.

The next morning I woke just before dawn to the sound of some sort of pounding on the outside of the cabin. My alarm turned to curiosity when I noticed that Washington was missing, and that none of the other guests seemed to be alarmed by the sound. Tossing on my coat, I stepped around and over the sleeping guests, or rather the grudgingly waking guests, and walked out into the grey chill of pre-dawn November.

Washington was pounding a nail into the wall beside the door with a stone for a hammer. When he moved his hand, I saw that the nail went through a hole in a brass panel or plaque. Another nail was already driven through a hole in the other end of it, and as I approached closer, and Washington stepped back to admire his work, I was able to read these words on the plaque, in finely engraved letters:

GEORGE WASHINGTON SLEPT HERE

"I have always thought," said Washington, "that gratitude ought to be promptly expressed, or it is as good as not expressed at all. In fact, there is a wise saying on that subject." The copybook came out of its pocket again, and Washington flipped through its pages. "I remember that it was... Oh, yes—here it is. 'Gratitude ought to be promptly expressed, or it is as good as a cucumber.' I may have miscopied that." He closed the book and slipped it back in the pocket.

By this time the rest of the party had risen, so after a breakfast of johnny cakes and salt beef, we set out on our way. I had brought the lightest possible pack, but it took four trips across the river to carry all the men and the baggage over. I admit that we were perhaps overly cautious, and the bag of dollars made every trip, owing to Parson Weems' reasonable insistence that it was unwise to leave Washington and the coins alone together on the riverbank, and Washington's flattering (if inexplicable) unwillingness to trust anyone but me with it. Once we had crossed the river, and the men had all assumed their burdens (Washington seemed to be carrying nearly his own weight in equipment), we set off along the Indian trail that crosses the Alleghenies.

"And what gives me the most satisfaction," Washington said as we walked, "is that I am almost certain that Irving has not followed us across the river."

"Who is this Irving?" I asked. "Forgive me for asking, but we heard you shouting his name in your sleep last night."

"Irving," he said gravely, "is my mortal enemy. For most of my life he has pursued me relentlessly, and I have no doubt but that he will continue to pursue me to the end of my life. He lives to deepen my sorrows, to blast my victories, and to hound me into an early grave. I am morally certain that Irving will be the death of me sooner or later."

"But how can one man be so thoroughly wicked?"

"Oh, Irving is not a man. Irving is a mule."

"A mule?" I asked incredulously.

"The most fiendishly devious and diabolically wicked mule ever bred."

"But—but what does he look like, this Irving?"

"Irving," Washington said, "is not visible in the

strict sense."

To this I could think of no reply, so we walked on in silence for a while.

The weather was turning colder as we crossed the mountains. We camped under a rocky overhang the first night; in the morning, Washington produced another brass plaque from his big clanking sack, but had the devil of a time trying to get his nails pounded into the rock, until I suggested that he apply the plaque to a nearby tree instead. This solution satisfied him, and we continued on our way.

So we went, crossing the Alleghenies in nine days and leaving a trail of brass plaques behind us. At the Allegheny River we made the trifling mistake of leaving Washington alone on the shore with the bag of dollars; but since we were obliged to make the crossing anyway, we suffered no serious inconvenience.

Eventually we reached the French post at Fort Le Boeuf, where we were received courteously by a lieutenant in a rather tattered uniform. Washington immediately brought forward his interpreter, Mr. Von Schloss.

"Guten Tag, mein Herr," said Mr. Von Schloss.

"I'm terribly sorry," the lieutenant replied, "but I don't speak a word of High Dutch. However, I have some rudimentary knowledge of the English tongue, if that will suffice."

"That will be suitable," Washington agreed. "I have a message from Governor Dimwittle that must be delivered personally to your commanding officer."

"If you will follow me," said the lieutenant, "I will conduct you to him forthwith."

We all followed Washington as he followed the lieutenant. The fort was a hastily constructed stockade, but one small building in the center showed considerably more effort than the rest. To this building we were conducted, and we waited outside while the lieutenant went in to inform his superior of our presence.

He emerged a few minutes later and told us, "Captain Hautain will see you now."

Washington entered, and we filed in after him, one after another.

The interior was sumptuously appointed, with carved chairs upholstered in fleur-de-lis patterns, fine tapestries on the walls, and a magnificent table whose marquetry top was covered with an array of pastries the likes of which I had never seen before in my life. Captain Hautain was standing before it in all his military splendor, his mustache perfectly waxed to a pair of dangerous points.

"Bonjour, mes amis!" the captain said cheerfully. "Vous avez quelque chose à dire? Bien! Mais maintenant, des napoléons!"

"Captain Hautain says that before you speak, you might like some of these pastries, which for some reason are called 'napoleons,'" the lieutenant said.

"Lieutenant!" the captain said sharply. "Vous êtes de trop! I will be the handling of these matter. —Gentlemen! Comme vous voyez, I speak English assez good."

"I'm grateful to you for your hospitality," Washington responded. "I shall come straight to the point. My name is George Washington, adjutant to Governor Dunwattle of Virginia, and I have come to warn you that you are trespassing on Virginian soil. It is imperative that you leave as soon as practicable."

"Ho! Virginian soil? It is a plaisanterie, oui? This is the soil of the Nouvelle France. Dites-moi, little adjutant fellow, if I should refuse the moving of my fort, yes?—then what would your Governor Denwallow do, hein? Comment?"

Washington appeared to be taken aback. He was silent for a few moments, and then he replied, "Well, I don't know. I had relied upon your honor as a gentleman to persuade you to do what was obviously the right thing. But perhaps you would like to hear Parson Weems preach first on the reasonableness of the Protestant religion."

"My text," Parson Weems began without further preamble, "is taken from the Letter of St. Paul to the Galatians, the second chapter, beginning with the—"

"Sacred blue!" the captain interrupted. "Away with your preachers of the preaching! I have the réponse for your governor, yes? You may tell your Governor Dingbattle that it is my irrevocable intention to keep toute la Nouvelle France, yes? Et par Dieu, if he comes here, je vais twiquer his nose! That is what il faut dire to your governor!"

An interval of silence followed this outburst; then Parson Weems suggested, "Perhaps you would like to read a small tract which I have composed, entitled 'Fifty Popish Falsehoods and the Answers Thereto,' which gives—"

"Hors d'ici!" the captain shouted. "And take with you your miserable heretical tracts! No napoléons! Allez-vous-en!"

The lieutenant was very apologetic as he escorted us to the gate of the fort. "Captain Hautain is of a warm disposition," he explained.

"I have done my duty, Lieutenant de Trop," Washington replied. "You have been most courteous, and I shall not forget your gentlemanly conduct. I have a reply to bring to my governor, and I shall bring it. For myself, I am certain now that Irving has preceded me here and has poisoned the mind of your captain."

"Irving, Mr. Washington?" the lieutenant asked.

"My mortal enemy. But I need not burden you with my personal affairs. Irving is no concern of yours. Farewell, Lieutenant de Trop, and may we meet again under more favorable circumstances."

So saying, Washington picked up his heavy sack of brass plaques, and the rest of us resumed our burdens for the long march southward.

The weather was now sharply colder, and flakes of snow were dancing among the brown leaves. Streams we passed were freezing along the edges, and at night the cold seemed to penetrate me with unusual power. Washington, however, made light of the difficulties of the journey, reminding me that, as it was written in his copybook, "When ladies are present, one can wait to use the chamber-pot." Our misery was compounded by a steady cold rain the third day, which soaked our clothes; and I think we might have frozen to death had we not found another natural rock shelter in which to build a fire.

We met a small party of Indians on the fourth day, and here our Indian traders proved invaluable to us. I directed them to ask the shortest route to the Allegheny River, which I intended to follow for some distance. Mr. Beadle addressed the Indian who appeared to be the leader of the group.

"Mr. Washington, him big chief in Williamsburg.

Him heap socially connected. Him going places. Him needum find heap quick trail to river of many waters."

"I'm sorry," the Indian replied, "but I don't quite catch your drift."

"He says," Mr. Gadelle explained, "that the little fellow over there is a very important man, and he needs to know the shortest route to the Allegheny River."

"Ah, yes, of course," the Indian replied. "Tell him to head straight for that gap in the hills down there to the southeast, and then the trail will wind down to the river. You can't miss it."

Mr. Gadelle turned to Mr. Beadle. "Him say, takum trail to hole in hill, walkum down to many waters."

"Heap much thanks," said Mr. Beadle.

Mr. Gadelle turned to the Indian. "He says he's very grateful to you."

Washington gave the four Indians a dollar each for their trouble, which seemed to please them; and indeed we found the trail exactly as they had told us. When we came to the Allegheny, which was much more boisterous this time, owing to the recent heavy rains, we continued downstream for a day and a half, until Washington came to a sudden halt in a grove by the riverbank.

I looked down at him to ask the cause of our abrupt stop, and saw the beads of sweat rapidly growing on his forehead.

"Hatchet," he whispered. "Hatchet... Hatchet... Hatchet..."

I looked around us. From the bark, I could recognize that the grove in which we stood was made up entirely of wild black cherry trees.

Suddenly Washington erupted. "Hatchet!" he shouted, dropping all his possessions with a loud clatter of brass plaques and drawing a hatchet out of his pack. "Hatchet! Hatchet!" With a mad gleam in his eye, he attacked the nearest tree like a man possessed. "Hatchet!" he bellowed as the splinters flew. "Hatchet! Hatchet! Hatchet! Hatchet!" So vigorous was his assault that the tree was felled in less than a minute. The rest of us scrambled to get out of the way as it fell, but Washington was still attacking it as it collapsed, and did not rest until the tree was reduced to a pile of logs of varying sizes. Then it was as if the devil had left him, and he sank down exhausted beside the logpile.

"Forgive me, gentlemen," he said after a few minutes' rest. "The...indisposition is usually under my control. But—so many cherry trees!" He took a few more heavy breaths, and then added, "I place the blame on Irving, of course."

"Well," said I, "since my plan was to build a raft at some convenient spot, and since we now have a ready supply of logs, I propose that we stop here and make our camp for the night, and then tomorrow we may assemble our raft at our leisure."

This proposal met with ready agreement; so we all set to work establishing our camp, and then retired early.

Washington woke us as usual with the sound of a brass plaque being nailed to a tree. Once we had fortified ourselves with some of our provisions, we set to work on the raft, using some stout frost-grape vines to bind the logs together. It took us most of the day, except for a few intervals of rest, during which Washington managed to empty his bag of dollars before anyone noticed what he was doing; but since we had to cross the river anyway, we thought the incident would be attended with little inconvenience.

With the raft finished, I proposed to camp there another night, making the crossing in the morning, when I hoped the river might be somewhat lower; but Washington insisted that time could not be lost, saying that it was of vital importance to inform the governor of the French response quickly. Thus, though it was already late in the day, Washington insisted on crossing the river immediately. We therefore piled our baggage on the raft and carefully launched it, using a long branch as a pole until the river became too deep, and then resorting to some improvised paddles.

The river was turbulent, and it took all our effort to stay on the raft and propel it in the direction of the southern shore. Nevertheless, we continued without serious incident until about two-thirds of the way across, when our raft was struck by a drifting branch, which knocked Washington's sack of brass plaques into the river.

Instantly and without a word, Washington leapt into the icy water. I shouted after him, but he sank like a brick. For some time—it must have been brief, and yet it seemed infinite—there was no sign of him. Our consternation may be imagined. Parson Weems began whistling "Lillibullero," as I would discover was his habit whenever danger threatened. But then, when we had already given him up for drowned, Washington appeared above the water and grasped the raft with one hand.

"Give me your other hand!" I called out to him. "I'll pull you up!"

"Impossible," he replied, in between loud gasps. "The other... the other hand...has...the sack."

"Let it go!" I begged him. "The plaques can be replaced!"

"A gentleman does not part with his honor!"

Casting about for some way to end this impasse, I leaned out with the branch I was using for a pole. "Get the sack on the pole!" I directed him, bringing it as near as I could to where I supposed his other hand must be. With much effort, he managed to snag it with the branch, so that Parson Weems and I could haul it aboard. Meanwhile, Washington's other hand was free, and Mr. Von Schloss and the two Indian traders were able to pull him up on the raft.

"Guten Tag, mein Herr," said Mr. Von Schloss, and we all concurred in the sentiment.

We landed a good mile downstream; but Washington, wet, frozen, and exhausted as he was, still insisted on walking that mile to retrieve his dollars before he would rest. Only when he had them safely back in his sack did he consent to make camp for the evening. Then we built a fire, and Washington carefully laid his copybook on a rock near the fire to dry. I think the poor man nearly froze to death in his wet clothes that night, but we never heard a word of complaint from him, save that, several times in the quiet of the night, he groaned out the name "Irving" in his sleep.

From there the next morning we followed the Allegheny down to the Forks of the Ohio, since the forbidding bluffs that lowered over the narrow strip of land on the south shore suggested to me that our most efficient route to the south would be by way of the Monongahela. At the point where the two rivers met, we stopped for a quick meal of the abundant game in those parts; and while we admired the magnificent view down the mighty Ohio, Washington was much taken with the strategic potential of the place.

"A fort here," said he, "at the confluence of these two mighty rivers, would command the only water route into the west, and thus keep the French from penetrating any further into my land."

"*Your* land, sir?" I asked.

"Indeed. My late brother founded the Ohio Company for the purpose of developing the western lands. As I inherited the estate, the land now belongs to me, from the Allegheny Mountains westward to the Russian Empire, assuming, as seems to be the case, that there is a connection between the western extremity of America and the eastern part of Asia."

"But how did your brother acquire it in the first place?"

"By forming the Ohio Company to develop it. You see, at present the only occupants of the land are Indians, who are savages, and the French, who are papists. The land thus belongs to the first civilized Christian gentlemen who are prepared to plant the seeds of true Christian civilization in it. A fort here will be but the beginning. At this commanding location I foresee a mighty city rising—a city whose position at the head of navigation into the west will give rise to undreamt-of prosperity—a city of titanic industries and globe-circling commerce—a city of gleaming towers and verdant parks—a center of learning and the arts—a city called Washington."

The remainder of our journey passed without any remarkable incident, and we reached my cabin early in December. Once again I offered the company my hospitality, which once again was accepted with thanks; but Washington and his party left so early the next morning that I was not able to bid them farewell. When I did come out of my cabin, I found the cherry tree by the river felled and a note stuck on the stump:

Mr. Gist—

My apologies for the state of your cherry tree, but the fit came upon me suddenly this morning. In compensation, I have left you ten Spanish milled dollars, if you will make the trifling effort to retrieve them from the opposite shore. I owe you a debt of gratitude that can never be properly repaid, but I shall see to it that the governor sends a handsome reward."

Yours, &c.,
George Washington.

Not too long afterward I received the handsome reward of which he spoke, in the form of a framed certificate headed "Valued Team Member" in elaborate blackletter, and signed by Governor Dinwiddie himself.

As for Washington, I had rather pitied the young man, imagining that the governor would be less than pleased with the outcome of the expedition, which had utterly failed in its object of displacing the

French. I had not reckoned, however, with Washington's mastery of the art of the dispatch. As soon as he reached Williamsburg, he wrote an account of his expedition that placed his own conduct—and, I understand, mine as well—in a very favorable light. Governor Dinwiddie was immensely pleased and had Washington's dispatch printed as a small duodecimo, which proved to be the most popular work ever issued by the press in Williamsburg, having sold upwards of eighteen copies.

So ended my first adventure with young George Washington, and I fully expected not to see the man again, at least for a great while. Momentous events were afoot, however, which would soon bring us together again.

CHAPTER II.

Expedition to Fort Duquesne.—Death of Jumonville and capture of French force.—Construction of Fort Washington.—Siege of fort.—Defeat and surrender.—Arduous march back.—I accept Washington's offer.

A scant four months later, Washington appeared at my door again. The man at my door was certainly the same Washington, but at the same time was different. For one thing, he was dressed in an even more splendid buff-and-blue uniform; but there was something else. In fact it came to me while he was greeting me: I was not looking down at him. The man had grown a good six inches. I was still somewhat taller than he was, but now his head came above my shoulders.

"Once again, Virginia has need of your services, Mr. Gist," he told me after we had exchanged greetings. "You were instrumental in the success of our recent expedition, and the governor and I would be honored if you would add your unrivaled knowledge of the western forests to our current enterprise."

"What little ability I have is at your service, Mr. Washington," I replied.

"Lieutenant Colonel Washington now. I received my commission at the beginning of the month. But ranks and titles mean nothing between friends, Gist, and I hope you will permit me to consider you a friend."

"I am honored, sir."

"And as your friend, let me tell you, do not belittle your own abilities. You have an instinct for difficult notions that has already proved very valuable. North, for instance. I have always had difficulty with that one, but you grasped it right away. I assume you have an equally good grasp of west, and those two notions together ought to get us to our destination."

"And what is that, if I may ask?"

"The Forks of the Ohio, Gist. My Ohio Company is constructing a fort there, and I have a commission from Governor Dingwoodle to reinforce it and take command. If, therefore, we may make use of your boat once more, I believe that we should be able to make quick progress by simply retracing the route that brought us hither the last time."

"The spring floods may retard our progress a little," I remarked, "but otherwise I see no reason why the expedition should not proceed quickly enough. How many are in your party this time?"

"One hundred sixty-three," Washington answered.

"One hundred sixty-three?" I stepped past him. Gathered in the clearing around my cabin was a motley assortment of militiamen, the sort of force for which the term "ragtag" might have been invented. I recognized none of them except, sitting on the stump of the cherry tree, the familiar figure of Parson Weems.

"Do you think we shall need to make more than one crossing with the boat?" Washington asked.

"It's possible," I answered.

"Then the sooner we start the better," said Washington. "There is a wise old saying..." He pulled out his copybook from his breast pocket and found a page in it. " 'A gentleman ought to avoid contradicting a lady if it is at all possible.' I live my life by these maxims."

After one hundred seven trips across the river and one hundred six back, we succeeded in transporting all the men and their equipment across the Potomac. We had proceeded only a few miles along the trail, however, when we were met by a small group of ill-dressed men coming from the other direction. One of them approached Washington immediately.

"Sir," he said, "I perceive by your blue-and-yellow uniform that you must be Lieutenant Colonel Washington."

"Buff and blue," Washington replied.

"Sir," the stranger said, "the French have taken Fort Washington."

"What do you mean?" Washington demanded in alarm.

"I mean that, whereas once we were inside the fort, with the French outside, now we are outside the fort, and the French are inside."

Washington looked grim. "This is disturbing news," he said.

"The French commander also said some very uncomplimentary things about you personally," the newcomer continued.

"What things were those?" Washington asked.

"I believe his exact words were, 'And you may tell that petit caniche Washington that if he should come here, je vais kiquer his derrière.' "

I asked the man whether this French commander were a certain Captain Hautain, and he answered that he believed that was the name.

Washington turned to address his men. "Men, the object of our expedition has changed. We are going to eject the French from the Forks of the Ohio, where they have ensconced themselves in the very fort we had been marching to reinforce. I must warn you all that we face a foe who does not scruple to insult us in a language we cannot understand. From that fact alone you may learn how wicked these papists are, and why it is necessary to expel them utterly from my —I mean our—land. I rely on every man's attachment to his country and to his Protestant faith, and to the large bonus Governor Damwadi will doubtless authorize when we are successful."

The men seemed pleased at least by the prospect of the bonus, and a few of them attempted something like a cheer, which gave Washington obvious satisfaction.

Indeed, I could already see the qualities that would make Washington such a renowned leader of men. The first night he showed himself a stern disciplinarian, sending several men to bed without supper for various infractions. Yet the men, if they did not positively love him, at the very least did not seem to be plotting to assassinate him.

Our progress was considerably slower than it had been in the previous expedition, owing to the larger number of men, the amount of equipment, and the many swollen streams we had to cross. Twice the mania came upon Washington, and an innocent cherry tree met its fate; but the third time was attended with momentous consequences.

It was a bright mid-morning in late May; the sunlight painted irregular splotches on the forest floor, and the air was pleasantly warm without oppressive heat. All at once Washington stopped in mid-stride, and I recognized all the symptoms: the perspiration, the gritted teeth, the trembling tension of every muscle. Beside him was a particularly fine black cherry, at least fifty feet tall, and in full bloom.

It was too much for him. In a movement too quick for the eye to follow, the hatchet came out of his pack, and chunks of wood began to fly in all directions. The air was filled with the heady scent of cherry sap, and Washington was shouting "Hatchet! Hatchet! Hatchet!" with each blow. The men, who by now had seen this performance at least twice before, did their best to remove themselves from harm's way; and soon the tree was toppling into the forest.

Suddenly there was a loud cry, followed by confused shouting. One voice, higher than the rest, penetrated the din: "On a tué de Jumonville!"

A French patrol! Washington quickly ordered his men into battle array, which was hard to distinguish from their accustomed random grouping, and led a charge toward the source of the shouting. I readied my musket, but by the time I reached the spot, the French were already surrendering to our overwhelmingly superior numbers. Their commander had been crushed by the falling tree, and he had probably died almost instantly; the rest of the French force numbered only nineteen, who were taken prisoner.

Having won this signal victory, Washington determined to build a fort immediately, reasoning that it would be easier to keep prisoners if he had a fort to keep them in. The Youghiogheny River being nearby,

I suggested that as a location; Washington, however, insisted on erecting the fort exactly where we stood, which happened to be a low and boggy meadow most remarkable for the proliferation of skunk cabbages in it. He immediately set the men to building, as soon as the French commander had been given a decent burial; meanwhile, he sent messengers back to Williamsburg with a dispatch giving a full account of the affair.

The fort went up quickly. We had all the logs we could desire: it was necessary only to find a grove of cherry trees and turn Washington loose on them, and we instantly had several days' worth of lumber. Washington himself drew up the plans for the fort, though I persuaded him to make some minor revisions. In particular, I thought that a museum, an opera house, and a university, while they would be of undoubted utility once we had established a more permanent possession of the Ohio country, might strain our resources at the present moment. Washington reluctantly agreed, but he would not give up his plan for a small theater for puppet shows. "I am passionately fond of puppet shows," he said. "And it is fitting that at least some accommodation should be provided for the muses at the very foundation of what will doubtless blossom into a great city, a beacon shining from the west—a city to be known, when it takes its place among the world's great centers of the arts and sciences, as Washington."

"Wasn't—" I began; but I stopped myself, supposing that no good could come of asking the question.

"You see," Washington continued, "it is fitting that the place be named after myself, since it is by *neces-*

sity that we have constructed it."

Fort Washington was nearly complete when messengers arrived from Williamsburg bringing a new commission promoting Washington to full colonel and officially ordering him to eject the French from the Forks of the Ohio by whatever means he thought appropriate. We were now on a war footing. Shortly after that, about two hundred men arrived, sent by Governor Dinwiddie as reinforcements. Washington immediately put them to work, some planting flower gardens, some laying out a green for lawn-bowling, and an elite detachment charged with mounting a puppet-show. The first performance took place the next afternoon; the plot involved the domestic arrangements of a husband and wife who settled their disputes by hitting each other with sticks. The men laughed riotously; Washington, however, watched impassively without so much as a smile through the whole performance, though he gave it his enthusiastic applause at the end.

That same evening, I dined with Washington, Parson Weems, and three of the officers, and we discussed the best means of surprising the French at their fort, which they had renamed Fort Duquesne.

"It seems to me," Washington said, "that our best chance is to march directly southeast."

"But the French are northwest of us," one of the officers objected.

"Precisely," Washington replied. "They will be expecting us to march directly to the northwest. But see what an advantage our Protestant natural philosophy gives us over the benighted papists. The most distinguished English philosophers and geographers assert that the earth takes the form of a sphere. If, therefore, we march straight to the southeast, we must eventually come upon the French fort from the northwest, taking the French completely by surprise."

The three officers stared without saying anything, and after a moment I perceived that they were staring at me. Parson Weems, too, was looking in my direction, with an expression compounded of amusement and anticipation.

"In theory," I said cautiously, "that strategy would indeed take the French by surprise. However, the advantage gained in surprise might might not be worth the loss of time. While we were marching, the French would have ample time to bring their reinforcements from Quebec, and no matter how surprised they were, they might be able to oppose us with overwhelming numbers."

"True," Washington agreed. "We might—heh—therefore be better—heh heh—better advised to—heh heh ha ha—to—ha ha ha—"

What had started as light chuckling rapidly grew into a gasping, choking fit of laughter. The officers were plainly alarmed, and even Parson Weems looked worried.

"Are you all right, Washington?" I asked, standing ready to offer my assistance.

"He hit—" Washington fell forward laughing and gasping, and for some time was unable to make any articulate sounds. At length he tried again: "He hit his—" More laughs, more gasping. Finally he was able to choke out a phrase: "He hit his wife with a stick!" He pounded the table with both fists, laughing and gasping with tears pouring down his cheeks; and it was quite some time before he was able to master himself sufficiently to resume the discussion.

Eventually it was decided that we should attack the French without delay by marching to the Youghiogheny and then down to the Monongahela, which we could follow to Fort Duquesne. It had the advantage of being a slightly more direct route than going around the world to the southeast, yet at the same time being somewhat more devious than marching straight along the Indian trail to the Forks of the Ohio.

In two days, all was prepared, and our whole force set out into the forest. Scarcely had we gone a mile, however, when a French force appeared before us and began firing. Washington's soldiers, brave to a man, soon discerned that the French had a distinct advantage in numbers, and were not afraid to show the broad expanses of their backs to the enemy, no matter how tempting a target they made. With laudable expedition, the entire force made it back to the fort in a few minutes.

The French soon had us surrounded, and as the bullets flew, Parson Weems began absentmindedly whistling "Lillibullero," as was his wont in times of danger.

Washington was glowing with battle ardor. "Do you hear those bullets whistling?" he shouted to me as he dashed from one side of the little fort to the other. "Believe me, there's something charming in the sound!"

I suppose I ought to have told him that it was Parson Weems he heard, but in the excitement there was no obviously appropriate occasion for conveying that information.

For most of the day we held out, but it was obvious that the French, with at least twice our numbers, must inevitably prevail. The officers and I agreed that a surrender upon terms was better than the loss of all our men. As I was, by this time, the one best acquainted with the humors of our commander, it fell to me to approach him with this unpleasant proposal.

"Washington," I said bluntly, "the officers and I believe it is time to discuss terms of surrender."

"Had enough, have they? Well, I shall be merciful. They shall have honorable conditions, since they have fought bravely."

"I meant *our* surrender," I said. I dreaded his reaction, but it had to be put as unambiguously as possible.

"Really?" He looked nonplussed for just a moment, and then said, "Oh, well—win some, lose some. Find a white rag somewhere, tie it on a stick, and let's get on with it."

I was quite surprised to hear him accept our advice with such good cheer, and I told him as much. But Washington merely pulled his copybook from his pocket and told me, "As the old saying has it, 'The other guests will be better pleased if you do not make slurping sounds when eating broth.' Such is the life of a soldier."

Within the hour, then, we were facing Captain Hautain himself, who could not contain his sneer. "So! It is the assassin of de Jumonville, yes?"

"If you mean," said Washington coldly, "that I led my men to victory against Mr. Jumonville's party, that is accurate."

"Victory! Plume de ma tante! You drop-ped the tree on him! I should have you executed for this thing alone!"

"We have come to discuss terms. If you do not wish to negotiate, we can go back to the fort and resume the battle."

"Oh, you shall be given terms, Monsieur Washington. When one has the little yapping poodle which chomps at the ankles, then one throws it the bone, yes? Eh bien, we give you the terms, and you allez-vous-en, and we are finis avec you." He looked back at one of his officers, who stood ready at a portable desk with a quill and paper. "Et maintenant, our terms."

The terms he dictated were simple and, I thought, for the most part generous.

"1. The Virginians will hand over their arms.

"2. The Virginians may march back with full honors of war.

"3. Colonel Washington will not name anything else in the Ohio country after himself for the space of one year.

"4. Colonel Washington will sign a paper stating that 'Washington n'est qu'un tout petit caniche qui jappe incessamment.' "

Before he affixed his signature, Washington was careful to ask, "What exactly do you mean by 'full honors of war'?"

"Sacred blue!" cried Captain Hautain. "I mean that you will be permitted to march out of la Nouvelle France without having to wear a sign on your back that says 'Kiquez-moi'!"

"That sounds fair," Washington agreed, and he

signed the instrument of surrender.

Our march back was a difficult affair. Washington himself was in surprisingly good spirits, and I wonder whether we should have made it back at all had it not been for his relentless good cheer. But we had no arms for hunting game. Once indeed Washington managed to crush a deer with a cherry tree, but we could not rely on such good fortune for the most part.

Parson Weems once congratulated Washington on his philosophical acceptance of defeat, but Washington saw nothing unusual in it. "Victory or defeat is almost immaterial," Washington explained. "The important thing is the dispatch. A well-written dispatch conquers all difficulties. As a wise man once said, 'Assistance promptly rendered to a lady purchases a good reputation for a gentleman in society.' " (This last was from his copybook.) "It is clear to me that Irving somehow warned the French of our attack, as there is no end to his malevolence; my duty, therefore, is to report to the governor, and to advise him on the next step to be taken to assure our ultimate victory, and the entire possession of the Ohio country for Virginia."

"What will you tell the governor?" asked Parson Weems.

"The truth, of course: that the entire expedition would have been lost but for the presence of mind and quick action of Colonel Washington."

We met a small party of Indians one day, and Washington attempted to trade with them for badly needed provisions; but the Indians made use of a gesture that consisted of bringing the thumb up to the tip of the nose, waving the fingers in the air, extending the tongue between the pursed lips, and making a sound like air escaping from a bladder, which in their marvelously expressive sign language signifies, "We are not inclined to treat with you at present." This was an indication that the local tribes were less favorably disposed toward us than they had been before, and that perhaps they were beginning to favor the French—a suspicion that would prove all too well founded.

At last we reached the Potomac, where, owing to our having considerably less equipment to carry, it took only one hundred sixty-five crossings in my boat to bring all 350 men across. Washington stayed on the north shore until the last man was across, and it was when we had already brought the second-to-last load across that we realized we had left Washington alone on the shore with the entire treasury of the expedition. I directed the men to take cover behind trees until the hail of dollars had subsided; then I went back across to pick up Washington, while the men collected the bonus to which they were doubtless entitled.

It was a little cramped, but I offered the men the hospitality of my cabin for the night, which they gladly accepted. In the morning, as they prepared to leave, Washington made an unexpected proposition.

"Gist," said he, "I have come to rely on your good sense and your expert knowledge of the cardinal directions. If you would consent to come with me, Virginia would be the better for it."

I thought it over briefly. We were now at war with France; I certainly could not rely on the security of my isolated cabin anymore, especially if the Indians had allied themselves with the French. But with Washington, I might have some small chance of affecting the outcome of that war. I gave him my hand and accepted his proposal.

"Splendid!" said Washington. "With Parson Weems' spiritual advice and your practical wisdom, the three of us should be more than a match for Irving."

CHAPTER III.

Washington a hero in Williamsburg.—Resigns in protest against English policy.—Life at Mount Vernon.—General Braddock takes Washington as aide-de-camp.—Washington's strategy.—Defeat.—Death and burial of Braddock.

WASHINGTON's dispatch, which he wrote on the way, preceded him to Williamsburg, and created a sensation in the capital. We arrived to find that Washington was celebrated as the hero of the age; the House of Burgesses presented a framed certificate to him, and, at Washington's insistence, to Parson Weems and me as well. Once again Washington had proved his mastery of the art of the military dispatch, and indeed he confided in me that he looked forward to a time in the distant future when the battles themselves would be unnecessary, wars being won or lost on the strength of the commanders' dispatches.

The colonel's fortunes seemed to be at a peak. Fortune, however, is not known for her constancy. Some weeks later, ships arrived from England bearing soldiers and officers. What had been an American conflict was now all-out war between England and France, and the officers newly arrived from England bore new orders which made the lowliest English lieutenant the superior of any colonial officer whatsoever. Washington's pride could not submit to such humiliat-

ing conditions. He resigned his commission and retired to his estate at Mount Vernon, whither Parson
Weems and I accompanied him. By this time, I should
mention, Washington had grown to exactly my height,
so that in the most literal sense we saw eye to eye.

Mount Vernon was certainly a different world for
me. Accustomed to a solitary life on the frontier, I
found myself on a plantation almost as big as the city
of Williamsburg, and one with a large population of
slaves. I must own that I had never thought much of
slavery one way or the other, as there had been no
slaves on the frontier; but the more I lived among
them, the harder I found it to understand how these
men, women, and children, with hearts and minds and
wills, could be accounted as property. Washington
seemed to accept the institution of slavery without a
thought; I supposed that a lifelong acquaintance with
it had taught him to accept it as part of the order of
nature. Not until many years later would I discover
how mistaken I had been.

Life at Mount Vernon was easy and pleasant—so
easy and pleasant, indeed, that I wondered what I was
doing there. Parson Weems spent his days composing
tracts against the papists. I read the books in Washington's library, walked along the river, ambled
through the gardens, and generally made myself comfortably useless.

Washington occasionally persuaded me to join him
in equestrian exercises. He was passionately fond of
horses, and he was a master of all departments of the
art of riding except for the matter of staying on the
horse. This latter skill eluded him, but he took his
tumbles good-naturedly.

The arrival of General Braddock put an end to our indolence. He came to Mount Vernon in February and was, of course, treated with Washington's wonted hospitality. After a generous dinner, we sat and shared a bottle of Madeira, and Braddock revealed the reason for his visit.

"Washington," he said, "your reputation has reached my ears, as indeed it has reached the ears of every Englishman, in the colonies or at home. The stunning success of your previous expedition could hardly have been improved upon, unless indeed you had defeated the French instead of the other way around. When I arrived in Virginia, I immediately inquired after you; and when I was told that you had resigned your commission, you can hardly imagine my disappointment, or my anger at the muddleheaded fools in London whose insulting ignorance deprived me of the finest officer in the colonies. I have come to rectify that grievous mistake. I am leading my army against Fort Duquesne in the spring. If you will consent to accompany me as my aide-de-camp, you will have your rank of colonel with undisputed authority over all officers in my army, myself only excluded. I believe that with your expert knowledge and brilliant strategic mind, we shall—um, we shall—um—"

The general stopped and appeared to be listening intently.

"Is something wrong, sir?" Washington asked.

"You didn't hear, just now, a sound that might possibly be described as 'lowing,' did you?"

"I don't believe so," Washington answered. He glanced at me and Parson Weems, and we both shook our heads.

"Ah. Very good," said Braddock. "One can never be too careful. As I was saying, I have no doubt that we shall defeat the French if I have you by my side, whereas I make bold to say that without you I do not believe it can be done. Will you accompany me?"

"My duty and my inclination both point to the same conclusion," replied Washington. "I must answer in the affirmative; it is my duty as a Virginian, and it is my pleasure as a soldier. This life of farming is an honorable profession for a gentleman, but for a soldier it must always seem a life of indolence and sloth. I have heard the bullets whistling, and believe me, there is something charming in the sound."

"Yes!" Braddock agreed vehemently. "Yes!—they whistle 'All in a Garden Green'!"

"In my last encounter, it was 'Lillibullero.' "

"Probably a difference in the North American climate." Braddock stood and extended his hand across the table. "Your hand, sir," he said. Washington stood and took Braddock's hand, and the agreement was sealed.

"One condition I should like to add," Washington said as he sat back down. "I should feel much more confident if Mr. Gist and Parson Weems came with us. Parson Weems' tracts are very effective weapons of the spirit, and Mr. Gist has an unrivaled understanding of the cardinal directions."

"Splendid!" said Braddock. "I myself have always had difficulty with east, so it will be very useful to have an expert on hand."

General Braddock accepted Washington's invitation to stay at Mount Vernon that night. Early in the morning, just after dawn, I was awakened by a loud pounding from very nearby in the house. Tossing a robe over my nightshirt, I dashed out into the hall to find that Braddock had procured a hammer from somewhere and was pounding a nail through a brass plaque into the door of his bedroom. He stepped back to admire his handiwork, and I was able to read the words engraved on the plaque:

EDWARD BRADDOCK SLEPT HERE

At this moment Washington appeared, already fully dressed, saying, "Good morning, general. I trust you slept well."

"Quite soundly," Braddock replied. "I hope I have not got you out of bed too early, but I wished to lose no time in expressing my gratitude for your hospitality."

"Not at all. I have always thought that gratitude ought to be promptly expressed, or—"

"—or it is as good as a cucumber!" Braddock finished, and the two men clasped hands. "Truly a man after my own heart!"

Several months still had to elapse before General Braddock's planed expedition. He wanted to wait until the spring floods had subsided before he set out. Washington occupied that time in having one of his slaves teach him how to play the mandolin, which he thought would give him a tactical advantage over the French; but as far as I know nothing ever came of this scheme.

We set out in June with a large force and a cumbersome baggage train, which meant that the Indian trail had to be broadened considerably to accommodate us. Washington was of less use in this regard than I had hoped. If a grove of cherry trees stood in the way, Washington could be relied upon to demolish them expeditiously; but it was vain to try rousing his enthusiasm for an oak or a maple or a beech, for no matter how valiantly he tried to bring on his mania, he was worth no more than any other soldier with an axe.

"Nevertheless," said Braddock one evening as he dined with the officers, "it is imperative that we make quick progress, both for the sake of expelling the French as quickly as possible and so that Jeremy will not catch up with me."

"Jeremy?" Parson Weems asked.

"My mortal enemy," Braddock explained.

"And this Jeremy," I asked, "wouldn't happen to be a mule, would he?"

"No, sir," Braddock replied. "An ox—the most fiendishly devious and diabolically wicked ox ever bred."

Parson Weems gave me a slight smile; Braddock's English officers pretended not to be paying attention.

Washington, however, responded immediately. "I know but too well what you mean. I myself have been pursued from my youth by a mule named Irving. He lives to deepen my sorrows—"

"—to blast your victories—"

"—and to hound me into an early grave. And yet—"

"—And yet he is not visible in the strict sense! By Jove, Washington, I was certainly right about you! It has been my observation, sir, that all great military commanders are pursued throughout their careers by

the forces of envy and malice, personified in malevolent invisible animals. It is almost the proof of a commander's greatness. Ah, Washington, what shall we
not accomplish together?—But for the present we require a plan, and for that I hope we may rely on your
wisdom."

"What wisdom I have, though I am very much your
junior in age and experience, is at your disposal," said
Washington.

"Then let us clear the table, bring in more
Madeira, and discuss our strategy," Braddock responded.

In a few minutes the table was cleared, and Braddock's officers unrolled a long chart consisting of a
circle marked "THERE" on the left, a circle marked
"HERE" on the right, and a long arrow connecting
HERE to THERE.

"We are here, and the French are there," Braddock
explained. "My plan was to take our whole army from
here to *there*, crush the French, and place ourselves
there. But I should like to have your opinion."

"If you will take my advice," Washington said,
"you will leave most of your force and equipment behind and attack the French with half our army at
most."

"An intriguing suggestion," Braddock remarked.
"What is your reasoning?"

"Elementary strategy," said Washington. "The
French will be expecting us to attack with a *large*
force. By attacking them with a *small* force, we take
them completely by surprise. The *Stratagemata* of
Frontinus are full of such ruses, which among the an-
cients invariably met with success."

"By Jove, what a remarkable military mind you have! Yes, I see how such a deception might put the fear of God into the papists! We shall put your plan into effect tomorrow morning."

Accordingly, the next morning the army was divided into two parts, the greater part remaining with the baggage train to follow the lesser part at a slower pace. Braddock and Washington and I would lead the lesser part over the Indian trail on horseback; Parson Weems, at Washington's insistence, came with us, but mounted on a docile old mule, as he did not consider himself much of a rider.

"I have named him 'Irving,' " Parson Weems confided in me.

"You are a strange and cruel man," I told him.

The main difficulty with making our expedition on horseback was keeping the general and the colonel on the horses. After a number of failures on the part of one of the officers, I took over the duty of helping Washington mount. After considerable effort, I would at last succeed in getting him up one side of the horse, only to hear him land with a thud on the other side. Braddock's valet had much the same trouble with his master. When we did get our two commanders mounted, we seldom went three miles without losing one of them on the side of the trail.

Each morning the camp awoke to the sound of the commanders nailing brass plaques to trees, and two mules were delegated especially to the task of carrying the sacks of plaques and nails.

We had made good progress by the beginning of July, and we were probably within two days' ride of Fort Duquesne when the French suddenly fell upon us.

They appeared all at once from both sides of the trail, and it was evident immediately that there were far more of them than there were of us. The battle might have been a rout from the beginning, except that we had no avenue of escape in any direction. Washington fell off his horse immediately, or rather his horse shot out from under him and tore away into the woods. (These words "shot out from under him," taken *verbatim* from Washington's later dispatch, would later be widely misinterpreted.) In the confusion, we did our best to get Washington mounted on another horse. Immediately he galloped off again, urging the men to press forward toward the west. A moment later, Braddock sailed by, urging the men, "Back! Back toward the thingy!"

"East?" I called out.

"Good man, Gist!" cried Braddock as he fell from his horse.

I ran to him and gave him what assistance I could.

"Do you hear those bullets whistling 'Lillibullero'?" he shouted as we mounted him on another horse. "By Jove, Washington was right!"

I had no heart to tell him that it was Parson Weems again, and at any rate he had already galloped into the thick of the battle.

With the two commanders giving opposite commands, and the French pressing in from all sides, the men were desperate, and the battle was turning into a massacre. Perceiving, however, a gap in the French encirclement toward the east, I rounded up the dozen men nearest me, and by our shouts we attracted more; and we were able to press through and begin what was perhaps too panicked and disorderly to be called a retreat, but was at least better than the massacre we were leaving behind us.

It seemed that we half-walked, half-ran for hours, turning as we could to fire on any pursuers. Eventually the French gave up the pursuit, since they could gain nothing by it. We began to regroup. I found that Parson Weems had made it on his mule, and somehow the two mules bearing the brass plaques had followed him. Washington was on foot and could not say where his horse had gone; but Braddock, who by the men's accounts had always placed himself where the fighting was thickest, was gravely wounded, borne on the back of some horse or other. When it seemed clear that we were out of harm's way for the moment, we stopped and let down General Braddock to see what could be done for him.

"Please don't waste your efforts on me," he told me when I had a look at his wounds—and indeed, though I said nothing, I could see that any effort would be wasted. "Washington will lead you back. Where is Washington?—Ah, there.—Washington, my boy, my career comes to an end here, but yours is just beginning. You know what to do now. Write the dispatch! The battle is lost, but write the dispatch and the war is won! It's not whether you win or lose, Washington —it's the dispatch!"

Those were his last words for some time. He slipped away from the conscious world for a quarter-hour or so, during which I told Washington frankly that there was nothing I could do, nor could our surgeon have done anything more had he not been killed in the battle.

The next time Braddock's eyes opened, he seemed not to see us at all. From the smile on his face, I believed he was already seeing sights far more splendid. He spoke only four more words: "I've beaten you, Jeremy!" Then he passed out of our world.

We buried Braddock under a great white oak. Washington gave a moving oration in memory of all our fallen; about Braddock in particular he said only, "The world has lost a hero, but I have lost a friend."

Then, as our fife-player whistled an appropriate dirge (he had lost his fife in the battle), Colonel Washington nailed a brass plaque into the oak tree above Braddock's grave:

EDWARD BRADDOCK SLEPT HERE

CHAPTER IV.

*Washington's greatest dispatch to date.—Parson Weems
and I are entrusted with an unusual commission.—
Seeking a wife for Washington.—Martha Custis.—
Washington's wedding and wedding night.*

In honor of his departed friend, Washington wrote
what was doubtless the best dispatch of his career so
far. It was true that he had returned with less than
half the force, and a considerable number of those
wounded; but upon reading his dispatch, Governor
Dinwiddie made Washington commander in chief of
the entire Virginia militia. In this capacity he partici-
pated in the capture of Fort Duquesne with General
Forbes. He disagreed with Forbes rather warmly on
nearly every decision; but in spite of ignoring Washington's advice, Forbes had the favor of fortune.
Washington's most vehement disagreement with the
general was over the naming of the new settlement at
the Forks of the Ohio, which Forbes decided to name
for the minister Pitt, though Washington reminded
him that there were men on the hither side of the
ocean who were more nearly concerned with the land
in question.

These disappointments temporarily soured Washington on the military life, and he used the excuse of
having been elected to a seat in the House of
Burgesses to resign his commission. In gratitude for

his service, he was made brigadier general at his resignation, for which his tailor made him a magnificent new buff-and-blue uniform. Washington indeed kept his tailor very busy: he had outgrown all his old clothes, and his tailor now measured him at six feet two inches tall.

I mention these momentous events only in passing because I was not part of them. On our return from the Braddock expedition, Washington had entrusted me and Parson Weems with a more delicate commission.

We had dinner at Ramsey's Tavern in Williamsburg the evening Washington personally delivered his account of the Braddock expedition to the governor, and it was over the Madeira after dinner that Washington brought up his plan.

"Gist, Parson," he began, "I am now at an age and in a position where it no longer behooves me to pass through life alone. It is true that my duties have kept me occupied hitherto, and I have not spent much time at home. But, as the governor intends to entrust me with the command of the entire Virginia militia, I cannot but assume that this French war will soon be brought to a successful conclusion; and then it will be time for me to cultivate the arts of peace. Now there is a wise old saying" (here he produced his copybook): " 'When yawning, put your handkerchief or hand before your face, and do not make a great show of the thing.' In other words gentlemen, it is time for me to find a wife."

The parson and I agreed that it would be an excellent idea for Washington to marry, and I asked him whether he had any suitable lady in mind.

"No," he answered, "and that is the commission with which I am entrusting you. No one knows my tastes and inclinations better than you two gentlemen. If you could find me a wife and have her ready for me by the time I finish the war, I shall be very much obliged to you."

Parson Weems gave me a glance with a raised eyebrow, signaling that he expected me to handle this matter. I boldly forged ahead.

"I'm not sure how I'd go about finding a suitable young lady," I began delicately.

"Oh, but that is the simple part. The ladies will come to you. I have a plan that cannot possibly fail. The Virginia Gazette in Williamsburg, and the Alexandria Gazette in the town of that name, print more than three dozen copies between them, reaching every estate of note in Virginia. A notice printed in those two papers will be read by every eligible young lady in the country, or by her father, which comes to the same thing. Let it be once printed, and, as I say, the ladies will come to you. You need only choose the most suitable candidate and present her upon my return for my approval—which will doubtless be forthcoming, since I have boundless confidence in you two gentlemen."

I glanced over at Weems, who indicated by his expression that he would prefer to have me continue to handle the discussion.

"And what would we say in this notice?" I asked Washington.

"You needn't trouble yourselves about that. I have already made up a suitable announcement, which I shall leave with you so that you may manage the business with the printers."

He reached into his breast pocket and brought out a folded paper, which I unfolded and read:

GENTLEMAN FARMER, tall, noted war hero, seeks extremely wealthy heiress or widow for marriage & investment purposes. I bear the rank of Colonel & own an estate bounded by the Potomac on the east & the Russian Empire on the west. I enjoy puppet-shows, equestrian exercises, fox-hunting, wrestling, fishing, dancing, billiards, bear-baiting, theater, cards, colt-breaking, duck-shooting, Madeira, & leading men into battle, but especially puppet-shows. You enjoy being rich, managing a large estate, entertaining important guests, & watching your husband invest your money in ambitious land schemes beyond the Alleghenies. Let us unite & profit from said union.

I passed the paper to Parson Weems for his perusal while Washington explained, "You will of course add the necessary information so that the ladies may reach you, and perhaps you will wish to make up a list of questions to ask when you interview them, such as 'How much land do you possess?' and 'How much per annum does it produce?' But I leave these minor details to your discretion."

"I gather," I said, "that the wealth is of paramount importance. But are there any other qualities you would look for in a wife? Physical qualities perhaps?"

"Well, of course she ought to be in good health. You might examine her teeth. I have been having trouble with mine, and a wife with bad teeth would be troublesome. I always examine the teeth before I acquire a horse, and I suppose the same precaution might be useful in acquiring a wife."

I tried to phrase the question a little more directly. "I mean to say, are there any physical qualities that attract you more than others?"

"Sturdiness," replied Washington. "Durability. Like any other household apparatus, a wife should be capable of reliable and continuous service."

I glanced at Weems, who reluctantly picked up the thread of the unraveling discourse. "He means," the parson began, and from there launched a detailed description of some of the things a husband might want from a wife, using some language that I might not ordinarily have wished to employ in company, but which was probably rendered necessary by Washington's apparent ignorance of the subject.

"My word!" Washington exclaimed when the parson had finished his discourse. "I had no idea marriage involved so many mechanical operations. But I should think that in this enlightened age we could dispense with those. The important thing is the land. Or the money, or any other forms of wealth. A happy alliance of fortunes is what I seek, and of course an eye for the proprieties in the entertainment of my guests. As for the rest, I rely on your wisdom and experience. It is the mark of a good commander to surround himself with capable men, and two more capable men than yourselves, gentlemen, I do not know."

Accordingly, while Washington was off on Forbes' successful expedition against Fort Duquesne, Parson Weems and I were managing the business of finding a wife for him.

We paid the printers to insert Washington's advertisement as he had suggested, adding a time at which candidates would be seen in the rooms we had rented next to the Gazette printing office on King-street in Alexandria. I had expected three or four ladies at most, and had been fully prepared to waste a day without seeing any. But when the appointed day came, I arrived at King-street to find a line of young and hopeful ladies stretching down to the docks, many of them accompanied by their fathers, others by brothers or elderly aunts. We had a full day of work ahead of us, for it seems that the word had got out that the gentleman farmer in the papers was none other than Washington himself, the most coveted match in the colonies.

Parson Weems and I divided the work between us. If one of us found a candidate who seemed to have the right qualities, she would be sent to the other to confirm the choice; then, out of that small number of best candidates, we would agree on one to present to Washington.

The plan was a sound one, but how much work it took to get us to that firm conclusion! With a feeling near despair I began questioning our first candidate and her father.

"What sort of fortune have you?" I asked her.

"My—" she began, but her father interrupted:

"A gentleman would not ask such a question."

I had to agree with him. I did not feel much like a gentleman that day, asking very personal questions of young ladies with whom I was not acquainted at all. Most of them had more hope than fortune. Some expected their beauty to compensate for their relative poverty; more than one of them could have had me for a husband that very day, but I was not the husband they were looking for. Twice I was threatened with a thrashing, once by a brother and once by an elderly but vigorous aunt.

The sun was low in the sky by the time we ran through all the candidates. Then it was time for us to speak to the ones we had set aside as possibilities. I had picked three for Weems to interview and he had left me five.

The first of Weems' choices came in alone. She was a very attractive woman, with emerald eyes and a copious mane of red hair; but her manner did not suggest an aristocratic upbringing.

"What sort of fortune have you?" I asked her.

"My pa's got a tavern on the Occoquan Ferry road," she replied.

"I see. And what do you think you have to offer Colonel Washington?"

"You want me to show you?"

After that interview I could see why she had appealed to Parson Weems, and I made sure to note the location of her father's tavern. But she had nothing of what Washington was looking for.

The next lady also came in alone, but in her dress and demeanor she showed every evidence of belonging to the old Virginian aristocracy. I began with my usual question:

"What sort of fortune have you?"

"Well," she began, "I have eight thousand acres outside of Williamsburg, three thousand five hundred on the..."

I traced the properties she mentioned on Farrier's

Map of the Province of Virginia as she rattled them off. The list went on for quite a while, and it was a nearly perfect fit. All the bits of Virginia that were not owned by Washington seemed to be owned by this woman. She had certain other sources of wealth, including a number of slaves, but it was the land that I knew would appeal to Washington.

"What is your family background, Miss..."

"Custis, sir—Martha Custis, widow of the late Daniel Parke Custis. My lamented husband left me comfortable; I mourned his passing, of course, but in the words of a wise old saying,—" here she produced a small ornately bound copybook and leafed through the pages. "Here it is: 'Do not read over another's shoulder unless asked to render an opinion.' " She closed the book, satisfied that she had made her point.

"Martha Custis," I said to Parson Weems after the last of the candidates had left.

"Martha Custis," he agreed. "But I hope you enjoyed the tavern wench."

When Washington returned to Mount Vernon as a brigadier general, therefore, Parson Weems and I were able to present it to him as our united opinion that Martha Custis was the wife for him.

"Splendid," said Washington. "Install her as mistress of the house at once, and we'll have no more worries on that subject."

"It might be best to meet her first," I suggested.

"No need for that. I trust you implicitly."

"Just for courtesy's sake," I insisted.

"Ah, yes, of course. A matter of civility and decent behavior. Thank you, Gist, for reminding me. Three months of frontier fighting have perhaps dulled some of my polish. Will there be any other little necessary civilities?"

"A wedding is usually expected," said Parson Weems.

"I had forgotten. Parson, I rely on you to deal with that aspect of the arrangements. Bring Mrs. Custis up to Mount Vernon, let's have a meeting and a wedding, and then my domestic arrangements will be complete."

Within a week we had Martha Custis at Mount Vernon, and Washington met his future wife for the first time. It was not five minutes before they had both pulled out their copybooks and were exchanging wise old sayings.

"And what especially pleases me," Washington confided to us later, "is that she has experience in the wifing business, so that she will be able to take up her duties immediately without any special training."

An alliance between two such illustrious families was inevitably a great event in Virginia society. All the Washingtons and Custises and Byrds and Randolphs and Taylors and Harrisons were there, and they all brought their copybooks with them, so that the air was thick with flying aphorisms. The wedding dinner was on a magnificent scale, and Parson Weems and I were among the guests who were privileged to stay at Mount Vernon that night—for even in those days, before Washington's additions, the house had generous accommodations for guests.

I rose early the next morning, and somewhat to my surprise found Washington already out walking in the herb garden.

"My word, Gist, what a happy man you've made

me!" he exclaimed as soon as he saw me. "Martha is everything I could have wanted in a wife!"

"It gives me great satisfaction to see you so well matched," I replied.

"To every young gentleman, I should certainly recommend taking an experienced woman to wife," he continued with a broad smile. "I'm sure you know what I mean, Gist."

"I have some idea," I said, returning his smile.

"She introduced me to a new sensation I had never before experienced, Gist!"

"Did she indeed?"

"She calls it cribbage. I wonder how I could have come so far in life without having been introduced to the game before."

Martha proved to be in every way the wife Washington needed and deserved. She was an accomplished hostess and a good manager, and the Washingtons' house became famous throughout Virginia for its hospitality. The next few years were a time of peace and prosperity for my friend Washington, and it seemed as though he had left military pursuits altogether and grown into his role of gentleman farmer. I took a house in Alexandria, not far from Mount Vernon, and Washington still found occasional uses for me. But it seemed as though his days of daring adventure were over. I had not, however, counted on the callous incompetence of the ministers in London.

CHAPTER V.

*Prelude to revolution.—Continental Congress.—Debate
over the generalship.—Washington chosen.—Siege of
Boston.—I meet Susanna.—Cannons brought from
Ticonderoga.—We seize Dorchester Heights, and control the harbor.—British evacuate.*

I SHALL pass over the next fifteen years without much
remark. Though the French and Indian War was successfully concluded on the Plains of Abraham four
years after Washington retired from active military
life, General Washington was remembered in the
colonies as the man who would have cleared the
French out of the Ohio country and won the war had
he not had the bad luck to be defeated each time he
attempted it. He was thus the only man in the
colonies whose reputation extended from Massachusetts to Georgia, and the great men of the age were
familiar guests at Mount Vernon. Washington expanded the house to accommodate entertainment on a
lavish scale. Wings were added with more guest
rooms; the kitchens were expanded so as to be able to
cook for a small army when the occasion demanded
it; and a small theater for puppet-shows was added in
the rear garden. Nothing was lacking that could possibly serve to keep Washington's guests comfortable or
amused.

In the meantime events were progressing that

would in the end lead to our rupture with the mother country and that revolution which would shower Washington with so much glory.

So habituated are we to thinking of Washington as the hero of the revolution that most of us have forgotten how little interest he took in the events leading up to it. The Intolerable Acts were quite tolerable for Washington; his wealth insulated him from the effects of arbitrary taxation, and the government of Quebec interested him no more than the government of the lunar regions. It was only when events began to take on a more martial character that Washington's interest was roused. News of the Boston Massacre filled him with righteous indignation, and he introduced a bill in the House of Burgesses prohibiting massacres of any sort in any town or independent city within the territory of Virginia—a bill that passed by a large majority, but which the governor refused to sign, describing it as disloyal to the crown, which, he said, retained a divinely instituted right to massacre citizens which no act of any colonial legislature could alienate. Positions were hardening on both sides, and men who had been peaceful citizens now began to speak openly of armed resistance. And if it came to that, there was, in Washington's mind, only one suitable leader.

By the time of the First Continental Congress, to which Virginia naturally sent Washington as a delegate, the General was ready in his own mind to take command of the colonial forces. Certainly he would have been the obvious choice had there been any colonial forces to take command of, but that one detail was lacking. The Congress therefore accomplished little. Washington indeed pressed it to adopt certain resolutions which had the effect of fanning the flames, notably the "King George is a fat Dutch slob" clause in the Suffolk Resolves, a clause which Washington regarded as essential to demonstrating the seriousness of the colonists' grievances. But these protests for some reason merely hardened the position of the king and his ministers.

Everything had changed by the time of the Second Continental Congress. By then the stirring events at Concord and Lexington had reached the ears of every American, no matter how remote, and with no real leadership or direction a large force of colonial militia had gathered around Boston, hemming in the British soldiers who occupied the city.

Summoned to that Second Continental Congress, Washington made it his first order of business to visit his tailor. He had grown to six feet ten inches tall, and thus required an entirely new uniform in splendid buff and blue.

This time Parson Weems and I accompanied Washington to Philadelphia. "Great events are doing, Gist," Washington told me, "and I have need of old and trusted friends. It may possibly be—I will not, of course, anticipate the decision of the Congress, but it may possibly be—that I shall be called to lead the forces investing Boston. In that case, I shall rely upon you to put affairs in order at Mount Vernon and then join me in Massachusetts."

This was my first visit to Philadelphia, the metropolis of America. Washington, of course, was familiar with the place; or at least he was familiar with the inn at which we stayed (where his chamber was already adorned with one of his brass plaques), the house where the Congress met, the tavern nearby, and a theater at which puppet-shows were regularly exhibited. The tavern was noted for a peculiar meal served on a small loaf of bread, consisting of thinly sliced beef mixed with onions and some green vegetable I did not recognize, with a certain liberal amount of cheese laid on top. Washington was much taken with the dish, which he consumed with his usual Madeira.

I attended the daily meetings of the Congress as Washington's adjutant, so that I was afforded a first-hand view of the momentous debates in which the future of North America was decided. Yet at the time one would hardly have thought that momentous debates were in progress. It is always only in hindsight that we can see history in the making; the dross is burned off in the flame of later events, and we remember only the gold. Most of the debates led nowhere. The question of independence was brought up by a few of the New England firebrands; the middle and southern representatives were altogether against the notion, regarding it as an absurd phantasy. Yet there was no real agreement as to what was the objective of the rebellion. Mr. Hancock, the merchant from Massachusetts, was of the opinion that the most desirable outcome would be a new system of taxation in which the burden of government was supported largely by the poor, leaving the rich free to invest their money in various enterprises that would enrich our country by enriching the owners thereof. Representatives from Georgia were certain that any equitable settlement would involve support for the silk industry. One of the gentlemen from Delaware believed that the rebellion would serve the divine purpose of inaugurating the millennial rule of the saints, but he usually kept to himself and indeed was encouraged to do so.

One thing, however was certain: that a rebellion of some sort was already in progress: and without some coordination among the colonies it was likely to end in disaster. The delegates seemed unanimously agreed that someone ought to take command of the volunteers currently besieging Boston, someone who represented the colonies acting in concert. But who might take that exalted position? Where might the Congress find a man who had both the military experience and the stature to meet the current emergency?

The delegates had picked June 15, 1775, as the date for a vote on the commander-in-chief of colonial forces. On the evening of the fourteenth of June, Washington insisted (against my gentle admonitions) on taking Parson Weems and me to see a puppet-show much like the one his men had mounted all those years ago at Fort Washington, but of course with more elaborate settings and puppets, and the addition of a crocodile to the dramatis personae. I found it amusing in its way; Washington took in the drama in almost reverent silence, with no visible change in his expression. I wondered whether he would suffer the effects of the show later that evening, but he seemed not to be affected at all.

The next morning, when the Congress met, Mr. Hancock began the debate with some abstract observations on the desirable qualities to be sought in such a commander as the Congress planned to appoint.

"Gentlemen," said Hancock, "it is to be noted that the soldiers—I scruple not to call these brave volunteers soldiers, though as yet few of them have any military experience—it is to be noted, I say, that almost all of them are from New-England, and indeed the greater part from Massachusetts. Now, this being the case, it is clear that they need one of their own to lead them: a New-Englander like themselves, and for preference a man from Massachusetts. It would indeed be most desirable to have a man of Boston, who would thus be intimately acquainted with the scene of the battle. Furthermore, our candidate must be a man already known to most of them, at least by reputation; and he must be a man universally respected by his neighbors. Now, it is a peculiar fact of the New-England character that wealth is the thing most likely to excite a New-Englander's admiration and approval. Our man must therefore be a man preeminent in wealth, which not only would give him the requisite reputation, but also could prove useful in meeting the needs of the army in an emergency. As for his name, it ought to roll of the tongue easily; and we ought not to diminish the importance of its beginning with a good sturdy letter, such as H, whose two uprights are solidly cross-braced for an appearance of stability that inspires universal confidence. I make no particular recommendations, of course; I merely state a few general principles by which this Congress may wish to be guided."

After this speech, Washington was recognized. He stood to his full height, which was more than a head taller than any other man in the room, and made sure the brass buttons on his buff-and-blue uniform were displayed to their best advantage. Then he began his discourse:

"Gentlemen, I thank the representative from Massachusetts for his observations. I must agree with him that, in the matter of personal wealth, our candidate must have a lot of it. I would add that it is desirable that such wealth be in a form that is not likely to lose its value in the vicissitudes to come: I am thinking particularly of land. I would suggest, however, that it is essential at this crucial moment to have all the colonies united. For this purpose it is necessary to show that we have set aside all considerations of sectional prejudice. What better way to demonstrate that we have not been influenced by local sentiment than by appointing a man who not only is not a New-Englander, but in fact has never even been to Boston? Moreover, such a commander's complete ignorance of the land, the town, and the waterways surrounding it will give him a fresh view of the situation, unhampered by the fettering influence of specific knowledge. Furthermore, it will be useful to have a man of such physical stature as to be able to make himself readily seen on the field. And of course it goes without saying that he must look well in his uniform; and all the better if he already possesses a suitable uniform, as in that case no time will be lost at the tailor's. In short, gentlemen, if you will take my advice, you will choose for your general a man who is tall, rich, Southern, well-dressed, and thoroughly ignorant. I hope these few remarks have been of some assistance to you in making your choice."

Washington resumed his seat to considerable applause, although what I had first heard as applause coming from the Massachusetts delegation proved to be the sound of Mr. Hancock slapping his forehead.

Mr. Carroll of Maryland then stood and nominated General Washington as supreme commander of the army of the United Colonies, at which turn of events Washington showed great surprise. Mr. Hancock, displaying signs of impatience or disgust, then rose and nominated Mr. Hancock. A vote was called for, and Washington rose to retire into the next room, saying that, as the vote concerned himself, he would not have the other members prejudiced by his presence, and would therefore occupy the time in brushing his general's uniform. I followed him, and thus was not present to hear the vote taken; but Washington was ready when the door opened and he was summoned to accept the commission of the Congress.

"I call every gentleman in the room to witness that I am not fit for this signal honor which you have bestowed upon me," he declared as he made his way to the center of the chamber.

"Well, in that case—" Mr. Hancock began; but he was ignored in the general press to greet Washington.

"However," Washington continued, easily addressing the whole assembly over the tops of the heads of the men surrounding him, "with the aid of Almighty God, and—heh—with the certainty—heh heh—that the brave—heh heh ha ha ha—the br—— ha ha ha ha ha ha—"

The laughing fit was now fully upon him, and Washington began whooping and gasping for air.

"He saw a very amusing puppet-show last night," I explained to the other delegates.

"The crocodile ate him up!" Washington wailed before he fell down in a chair, kicking his feet in the air, unable to speak for quite some time. The chamber echoed to the sounds of Washington's laughter, the applause of the delegates, and a rhythmic thumping, which I found to be coming from Mr. Hancock, who had grasped the ledger in which the minutes of the sessions were kept and was busy smacking himself in the face with it.

Washington set off for Boston the next morning. I did not accompany him; instead, as we had planned, I rode back to Mount Vernon to make a few final arrangements for Washington's extended absence. Mrs. Washington was quite competent to manage the estate, but Washington trusted me alone to bring him certain necessities, among them a dozen pairs of his favorite silk underwear.

It was thus some weeks before I arrived at Boston, or rather at Cambridge across the river, where Washington had made his headquarters. The city was still occupied by the redcoats, but the colonial volunteers held most of the land around the city. The British could not get out by land, but they could supply themselves by sea. Under those conditions, the siege could go on till the day after Doomsday.

As soon as I identified myself, I was conducted to the house that served as Washington's headquarters. I entered and was left in a small front parlor warmed by a generous fire.

Here I expected to meet Washington, and I was rather surprised when, instead of the General, a young woman came in and greeted me:

"Mr. Gist?"

She looked about twenty at the most, with a complexion of pure dark walnut, jet-black hair, dark eyes that blazed in the firelight, full lips that invited thoughts of what they would feel like against mine. I thought she was the most beautiful woman I had ever seen in my life, all the more so because she was dressed in a militia officer's uniform, which molded the shape of her figure in a way that emphasized all the features a man likes best in a woman.

Had Washington taken a mistress? No, the idea was absurd. But who was she?

And then it occurred to me that she had spoken to me, and I ought to answer her.

"Yes—Christopher Gist, Miss..."

At that moment Washington burst into the room and seized both my hands. "Gist, my dear friend! How good it is to see you and my underwear. I see you've met Phillips."

He was obviously referring to the beautiful young woman in military dress. "Yes. Yes, we were just introducing ourselves."

"Invaluable man, Phillips. He has a mind for military problems. You'll like him when you get to know him. Now let me have a pair of my underwear. You can hardly believe what I've been reduced to wearing up here. There we are! I'll be right back."

He left the room holding his underwear out in front of him, ducking his head to avoid banging it on the lintel.

The young woman waited until she heard another door close. Then she turned back to me.

"The General believes I am a white man named Phillips. You may attempt to tell him otherwise. Perhaps you will have better luck than I had."

"But you're really—"

"Susanna, Mr. Gist."

"Susanna Phillips?"

"Just Susanna."

"And you are a, um, a..."

"A free woman, sir."

"And no one else has remarked on the, um, the fact of, uh..."

"The men don't like to contradict the General, Mr. Gist."

I could certainly see the wisdom of that policy. It was not that there was any danger in contradicting Washington, who was the most affable man in the world; it was simply that contradicting him was a task like that of Sisyphus, but far more fatiguing. "The men are right. He'll get no contradiction from me. But how—I mean, what brought you into the continental army in the first place?"

"My uncle, sir—I mean, not really my uncle, but I called him that, and I loved him, and the redcoats killed him in the Massacre, when I was a girl of twelve. And now that I have the chance, sir, I thought I might return the favor. Many times over, if I can manage it."

At that moment my old friend Parson Weems appeared in the doorway. "Gist! You've made it. How are things at Mount Vernon?" He made his way to the fire and opened his greatcoat as if to absorb all the heat from the flames.

"Mrs. Washington is in good health and keeping the house in order," I replied.

"Very good. I see you've met Susanna. Our friend the General thinks she's a remarkable man."

"So I'm given to understand."

"I'm beginning to think he's right," Weems added,

with a smile for Susanna, which I noticed she did not return.

"How has the siege been going?" I asked—"if 'siege' is the right word."

"We have the redcoats penned up," Parson Weems answered. "They are confined to Boston and such places as they can reach from the harbor, which is to say England, Europe, the Americas, Africa, Asia, and the islands. But, by heaven, they can't get to Cambridge."

"And has Washington done anything to change the situation?"

"Well, he sent an expedition to a pencil-factory in the wilds of New-York."

"New-York? What in heaven's name has that to do with the siege of Boston?"

"Susanna gave him the idea," Weems said with a wry smile.

I turned to the dark beauty, who explained, "There was a certain young officer who was too...energetic. He was constantly meddling in the conduct of the siege. So I thought his energy might best be expended in an unexpected attack on an important British installation in the interior."

"Ticonderoga supplies the pencils for all the British forces in North America," Weems explained.

"If Arnold is half the brilliant commander he thinks he is," Susanna continued, "an American victory will fill the whole army with enthusiasm. If he fails, we shall hear no more of him. Either way, he will be *there* instead of *here*."

"I see," I said, and I had to admit the idea seemed to be well thought out. "And you made that statement to General Washington?"

Parson Weems laughed. "Not precisely, eh, Susanna?"

Susanna glanced down at the floor. "The general may possibly be under the impression that Ticonderoga is a suburb of Boston," she said rather quietly.

"Clever man, our Susanna," Weems said with a smile.

Washington now came into the room; but as he had forgotten to duck under the lintel, he was rubbing his forehead. "They build houses smaller than they used to," he complained. "But at least the underwear situation is rectified." He turned to Susanna. "What is the news from the troops?"

"They are cold and miserable and bored," she replied.

"Good man, Phillips. See what you can do for them."

"Yes, sir," Susanna replied, and she left the room. We heard her putting on her coat and going out the front door. Then Washington spoke in a more confidential tone.

"Gist, Parson, I've sent Phillips away because I wished to speak to you about him privately. You've known him as long as I have, Parson, and Gist, you've seen enough, perhaps, to be able to render an opinion. I've been worried that there's something not quite right about him."

"Really?" I asked warily, and at the same time Parson Weems said, "Indeed?"

"He works so hard that I hate to say anything to him," Washington continued, "but I've been concerned for some time. Does he look pale to you?"

Weems and I looked at each other silently for a few moments.

"Not...particularly," I replied at last.

"Not more than usually," Parson Weems agreed.

"I wouldn't say 'pale' exactly," I added.

"Some men have naturally pallid complexions," said Weems, but I tried to signal him that he was perhaps going too far.

"Thank you, gentlemen. I may be imagining things," Washington said, "and indeed I hope that is the case. I feel better having the opinion of two trusted friends. Mr. Phillips has proved so useful that I naturally worry about his health, but you have reassured me."

That night I shared a room with Parson Weems, who snored abominably. Washington had suggested putting me up with young Phillips, a temptation I resisted on the grounds that, if his health indeed was delicate, he ought to have a room of his own.

The next morning came a great sensation: that proud young officer Benedict Arnold had returned from Ticonderoga covered with glory, bearing with him enough pencils to supply the colonial forces indefinitely, and, what was just as important, the cannons the British had been using to defend the place.

"Now," Washington said later on, when he was having dinner with Susanna, Parson Weems, and me, "we have the means to evict the British from the city. With these cannons, we can level any hiding places and leave the redcoats no shelter whatsoever."

"That would have the effect of destroying Boston," I remarked.

"True, but it may be necessary to destroy the city

in order to save it."

"The cannons need not be trained on the city," said Susanna. "There is a hill at Dorchester Heights with a commanding view of the harbor. If the cannons were brought up to the top of the hill, they could be trained on the harbor, and the British would find it impossible to withstand our siege."

"An interesting thought," Washington replied, "but it seems to show your inexperience. I have seen cannons in operation. They are very effective against solid objects, but against the liquid element I believe they would have very little power. When a hole is made in water, you see, the water on all sides rushes in to fill the gap, and in a manner of speaking the body of water repairs itself instantaneously. I do not believe a cannon could do any permanent damage to the harbor at all."

Susanna was looking downward with her fingers on her temples, as if suffering from a headache; but she spoke in a civil tone. "I was thinking of the ships *in* the harbor, General."

"The ships?"

"The redcoats can stay in Boston forever as long as they can supply themselves by sea. If we make it impossible for their ships to come and go safely, the British will not be able to hold out very long."

"Oh," said Washington, looking puzzled. "But how do we make it impossible for the ships to come and go safely?"

"By blasting them to splinters with our cannons!" Susanna exclaimed; and then, more calmly, she added, "sir."

"Ah, I see." And then Washington's face lit up.

"Yes! My word, I do see! Well done, Phillips. We'll give it a try."

Immediately the order was given to occupy Dorchester Heights, and soon our cannons were making quite an impression on British shipping.

"And now what do we do?" Washington asked Susanna as we stood on the heights looking down into the harbor, which for the moment was singularly free of British ships.

"Nothing," Susanna replied.

"Nothing?"

"Nothing. When the British ships come in, we fire on them. But otherwise we wait and do nothing. The British will realize the impossibility of their situation, and they will either try something desperate and stupid, or they will simply leave—and we shall let them leave—and the city will be free. All we have to do is—nothing."

"Yes!" Washington agreed enthusiastically. "The 'nothing' strategy, which worked so well for General Forbes. You remember, Gist—oh, no, you weren't there. But you heard the story. The French ran away and burned their own fort without a fight, all because General Forbes did nothing. Well, gentlemen, if nothing worked for Forbes, perhaps it will work for me as well. We'll try nothing."

So we did nothing. I spent some of that time getting to know the charming Susanna better, but I was not aware of how much she had charmed me until one evening Weems came into the room we shared with a blackened eye that was painfully obvious even in the dim rushlight.

"What happened to you?" I asked.

"I tried my luck with Susanna," he replied. "Apparently fortune did not favor my attempt."

I suddenly found it difficult to control my rage, which is a very unusual condition for me. "Weems," I reminded him, "you are a man of the cloth."

"The cloth does not always cover the man," said Weems.

"You insulted a lady!"

"She's only a negress."

Suddenly I was much closer to him. "She wears the uniform of the Virginia militia! As far as you are concerned, she is an officer and a gentleman, and you will treat her as such, or by God, Weems—"

I stopped. I realized I had been shouting in his face. I backed away.

"I'm sorry, Weems."

"Apparently the subject interests you warmly," he said with an infuriatingly wry smile.

"I will not mention it again."

"You were merely following your chivalrous instincts."

"And you will apologize to Susanna at the earliest opportunity."

"Now, really, Gist—"

"You will apologize to her," I repeated, and I think he could see that I meant it seriously.

"As you say," he replied with a sigh of resignation. "Since you take such a personal interest in the matter, however, I have a bit of advice for you. Beware of her right fist. You'll never see it coming until it's too late."

Not long afterward, the British evacuated Boston. Washington rode into the city in triumph.

"My word!" he told Susanna, "this 'nothing' strategy certainly reaps abundant benefits. I ought to have tried doing nothing a long while ago!"

CHAPTER VI.

Washington declares for independence.—Susanna and I travel to Philadelphia.—Jefferson drafts the Declaration.—Debate over spinach, slavery, and silkworms.— Mr. Rodney decides the question of independence.— The Declaration signed.

By the spring of 1776, Washington had assumed a stature well above that of any other man in the colonies, and the best tailors in Boston were kept busy making him a new wardrobe. He was measured at seven feet seven inches tall, and we were beginning to have to make certain adaptations to accommodate his unusual height, though always discreetly, so as to avoid dwelling on what might well be a sensitive subject with the General. We found a house with high ceilings for his headquarters, and for his mount we procured a sturdy carthorse of the largest dimensions, which was docile enough that, provided he did not attempt any difficult feats of horsemanship, such as trotting, he did not often fall off.

Meanwhile, the victories at Ticonderoga and Boston had changed the perception of the conflict throughout the colonies. It was a war now, and it seemed possible that it might be a war that could be won. The popular sentiment now favored a complete and permanent break with Great Britain, and Washington himself had come around to the idea and now embraced it enthusiastically.

"The time has long passed," he declared at dinner one afternoon, "when we could expect King George and his ministers to see their own folly and redress our grievances in a forthright and responsible manner. We have grown too distant from England for that; we have our own interests, and I may be so bold as to say that we have preserved the true spirit of English government, which has been lost in the mother country. I believe it is our destiny to found a new kingdom on the American continent, a kingdom which, as it is already greater in extent, must soon be greater in wealth, population, and power. Of course it will be necessary, in order to have a kingdom, that we should have a king."

"Perhaps one of the exiled Stuarts," Parson Weems suggested.

"But the last Stuart king was even more tyrannical than George III," I objected.

"That is true," Washington concurred. "I believe that the founder of a new American dynasty ought to be one of our own people: a man born on our soil, and one widely known in the colonies; a man of stature, you might say, who would naturally be looked to as a leader. It might also be of use in easing our transition to full independency if he bore a name already in accustomed use as the name of kings, so that it came naturally to the tongues of the people. A good uniform would also be a desideratum, as kings look well in uniforms. I say no more for the present, but I shall be ready with my suggestions when the time comes."

Much later, after Washington had gone upstairs to bed, Susanna asked, "Shall we really trade one imbecile for another?"

"Washington," I said rather too warmly, "is a man with a great heart and the most thoroughly honest nature I have ever known. If we must have a king, let it be such a king as that."

"Besides," added Parson Weems, "imbecility has never been thought a detriment in kings."

"But why must we have a king at all?" Susanna asked, and to that I could think of no very good answer.

The next day we received messengers from Philadelphia, who informed us that the question of independence was to be brought up in the Congress. It was not possible that Washington should leave the command of the army, but he did earnestly desire to have a report of the debates.

"You go, Gist," he told me. "There's no one I trust more than you, and if I cannot be spared, I should at least like to have you there to hear what is said, and to make my sentiments in favor of independency known."

"I am honored by your trust," I replied.

"Take Phillips with you," Washington added. "He has a sharp mind, that man. He might be useful if difficult questions come up, especially in matters of arithmetic. I have found him extraordinarily useful in matters of arithmetic, especially when the numbers go above twelve. I am not very good at numbers above twelve."

All at once I was paralyzed by indecision. If I had to go to Philadelphia, how much more pleasant it would be to have the divine Susanna with me! Yet it would expose me to great and terrible temptations of the sort Parson Weems had not been able to resist. Ought I not, therefore, to suggest that she stay with Washington? But that would deprive me of her company, and of the possibility of yielding to temptation, which could be very pleasant if Susanna were equally tempted. If not, I might end up with a blackened eye, as Parson Weems had done, and if I behaved as he had behaved then I would certainly deserve that fate.

Thus buffeted by conflicting desires, I said nothing; and because I said nothing, Washington's will was done.

We were to go to Philadelphia by ship—something of a risk, but not too much of one, as the British did not yet have the capacity to blockade our ports. I would like to tell you a thrilling sea-tale, but in fact we had calm weather and no danger of any description, except the danger to my self-mastery incident to traveling with a lady whose charms seemed to captivate me more every hour. I behaved as a gentleman the whole way, and I still regard that as one of my proudest achievements.

Susanna, of course, excited some comment, the more so as she was still in uniform; but the letters from General Washington answered all questions. If the General stated that a colored woman was a lieutenant named Phillips, then so it must be.

We arrived in Philadelphia to find the city miserably hot. Susanna and I lodged at the same inn where Washington and I had stayed months before, and indeed Susanna slept in the same room Washington had occupied. The innkeeper was a little baffled by the arrangement: he accepted the letters from Washington as proof enough of her right to wear the uniform, but still persisted in assuming that I must have brought her along for immoral purposes. I fear I must have used some language with him that was strong in proportion to the temptation I was resisting, for the poor man after that was never quite able to decide whether to treat her as an officer or as a lady. But at any rate he treated her with respect, mingled with a certain amount of fear.

At dinner we discovered that two of the members of the Congress were staying at the same inn: Mr. Harrison and Mr. Jefferson, both from Virginia. When he saw the divine Susanna, Mr. Jefferson gave obvious signs of admiration; I thought his eyeballs might tumble out of his head, so eagerly did he devour the sight of her. My jealousy was naturally inflamed, but as I had made no declaration to Susanna, I could but watch and fume silently, meanwhile treating Jefferson with scrupulous, if not over-scrupulous, politeness.

"I believe the question will be settled in the next few days," Jefferson said when I asked about the debate on independence. "We require a unanimous vote; Mr. Franklin has some clever saying about the necessity for unity, which I have forgotten at the moment, though it has something to do with hanging, believe it or not, but that's Franklin's sense of humor. At the moment Georgia and Delaware are holding out. It goes without saying that Massachusetts and Virginia have stood for independence from the beginning. The other colonies have fallen into line one after another, but Georgia is waiting for the silkworm issue to be addressed before making a decision. As for Delaware, I believe the whole colony has no more than three men in it, and the two sitting in the Congress now are of opposite opinions. The third went home with a headache some time ago, but we may have to send for him to get a decision from Delaware. Meanwhile, I have been asked to draft a proclamation or declaration showing the causes why we must break the bonds which connect us with England, on which I should be happy to have your opinion."

"Oh, I'd be very interested in seeing that," said Susanna.

"Dear lady, nothing would delight me more. If you would come to my chamber, we can peruse it together as long as we like, and—"

"Why don't we bring it down here to the front parlor?" I suggested quickly, "—so that the three of us have room to peruse it together."

Jefferson was visibly disappointed when Susanna eagerly assented to my suggestion, but it was too obviously reasonable to admit of any objection. Accordingly, after dinner, we sat in the parlor and heard Mr. Jefferson read the text he had written, after which he invited our opinions and suggestions.

"The beginning might perhaps be a little more dignified," I said.

"Do you think so? I wondered about that. I was aiming for a colloquial directness, but you say that 'When you've got to go, you've got to go' leans too far in that direction?"

"It ought," said Susanna, "to begin with a few resounding phrases, easily remembered but impressive and tending to emphasize the seriousness of the occasion."

"How about something like 'We, the people of the thirteen United States of America,' and go on from there?"

"I don't think that quite fits," said Susanna. "It sounds well, and you should keep it in mind for something in the future, but for the present we need something that places us firmly in the flow of history, so that the world knows that we are justified not only by facts but by precedent. Something like 'When in the course of events' to start with, and then a brief statement of what we are compelled to do."

"By heaven, dear lady, I think you've hit on something there," Jefferson said, hurriedly dipping his quill in the ink-pot and scribbling her suggestion at the top of his first sheet.

"You have quite a list of complaints against King George," I remarked.

"Yes, it seemed necessary to make the list long and detailed, so that we should not seem to be revolting for light and whimsical reasons."

"Some of them," I continued, "I do not quite understand. For instance, 'He has made us eat spinach.' "

"*Somebody* made me eat my spinach," said Jefferson. "Mother always said, 'Eat your spinach for King George.' "

"Ah, I see."

"I don't like spinach," Jefferson added.

"What about the slave trade?" Susanna added.

"The slave trade?"

"The slave trade," she repeated, her dark eyes blazing; "that wicked and murderous trade in the human species, which condemns the more fortunate of its victims to a miserable death on unspeakably filthy ships where they are stacked like cordwood, and the less fortunate to a life of unending servitude under the whip of a master whose cruelty is unchecked by law, and against whose foul lusts the women have no defense; the children from such unions, the only consolations afforded to the victims, being ripped from the arms of their wailing mothers and callously sold to buy a few trifling luxuries for the man who calls himself their owner. What have you to say to King George about the slave trade?"

"By God, madam, I shall have something to say about it!" Jefferson said, his pen scratching frantically. "Where, madam, did you learn such eloquence?"

"My father, sir—my adoptive father, for I was left on his doorstep—was a minister of God, with a library of a few well-chosen books. One of them was the Bible."

"Oh, yes—the Bible. I've always meant to read it, but every time I start I think what an awful lot of words there are to get through. I have always thought it would attract more readers if it were condensed into the form of a small octavo of a few dozen pages. When I have leisure, I shall undertake the work."

Fatigued by our journey, Susanna and I both retired early. The next morning I woke and dressed and came downstairs to find Jefferson nursing a blackened eye. I said nothing, and he was not as garrulous as he had been the evening before. When Susanna came down, and Jefferson was momentarily out of the room, I asked her, "Did Mr. Jefferson pay you a visit last night?"

"I took care of it," she replied. She had no more to say on that subject.

As General Washington's representatives, we were allowed to be present at the daily sessions of the Congress as silent observers. On that first morning, Jefferson presented his draft declaration, and debate began with the first line.

"I think you ought to specify what kind of events you mean," said Mr. Whipple.

"What *kind* of events?" asked Mr. Jefferson.

"Say, 'When in the course of *human* events.' That makes it clear."

Mr. Harrison interrupted. "Really, Whipple, what other kinds of events would we be talking about?"

"Well, equine events, for example. Or canine events. Things happen to horses and dogs all the time. It's not just humans who have events."

"Do you really want to complain that King George has trampled on the rights of horses and dogs?" asked Mr. Harrison.

"No," said Mr. Whipple. "I wish specifically to remove the ambiguity and make it clear that we are *not* concerned with the rights of horses and dogs."

"The word has been added," said Mr. Jefferson. "When in the course of *human* events."

"Which is absurdly redundant," Mr. Harrison grumbled.

"But it will do," said Mr. Jefferson.

"*Why* are we not concerned with the rights of horses and dogs?" asked Mr. Gerry; but he spoke in a soft voice, and thus was ignored as Mr. Reed rose to speak.

"Delaware," said Mr. Reed, "has not declared for independency; but if she were to do so, her representatives could in no wise accept this condemnation of spinach-eating. Spinach-growing is one of our two main industries: that and picture postcards with sand dollars on them are the twin pillars of our prosperity."

"It is removed, Mr. Reed," said Mr. Jefferson, striking a line through the offending clause.

"Look here, Jefferson," said Mr. Rutledge, "what's all this intemperate language about slavery?"

"It hardly seems intemperate to me," said Jefferson. "The language indeed seems hardly adequate to describe the human misery inflicted by the institution of slavery."

"But you make human misery sound like a *bad* thing," Mr. Rutledge complained. "Human misery is the foundation of our happiness in South Carolina. Misery is the divinely ordained condition of the African, so that by God's providential arrangement the white man can have the leisure to glorify his Creator by drinking juleps and playing whist. That is why he gave the African such a hideously dark complexion." And then, realizing that there was a lady present, he nodded to Susanna and said, "No offense intended, madam."

She gave him a smile that would have frozen a volcano.

Here Dr. Franklin stood and, with an eye on Susanna, began to speak: "I wish to register my strong objection to Mr. Rutledge's characterization of the African complexion as 'hideous'—a characterization rendered nigh incomprehensible by the ample evidence to the contrary we all have right before our eyes. It is time to end this curse before it blights the hope of our nascent confederation. A stitch in time saves the mime. I support the condemnation of slav-

ery and the slave trade as Mr. Jefferson wrote it, and I
further condemn slave-owners as depraved and de-
bauched men whose wickedness makes them hardly
less than devils incarnate. No offense intended, Mr.
Rutledge."

Mr. Wythe spoke next: "But see here, Jefferson,
you're a slave-owner yourself."

"Am I?" Mr. Jefferson responded with some surprise. "Why, so I am. I have so little to do with the
slaves, you see. I have a manager for that purpose."

"And who is your manager?" asked Mr. Rutledge.

"Oh, one of the slaves takes care of that. Well,
then, gentlemen, I think we can strike the slavery
clause, can't we? Let's move on to more important
questions."

Susanna's right hand was clenched into a fearsome-
looking fist, but she kept her seat.

Mr. Gwinnett spoke up. "The colony of Georgia is
not likely to declare for independence unless the silkworm issue is addressed. We suggest a clause, perhaps
replacing the slavery clause, along these lines: 'He has
failed to send the right species of mulberry for our
silkworms.' "

We returned from the day's debate somewhat
dispirited, but nevertheless appeared dutifully to hear
the next day's session, which was taken up mostly
with the silkworm question, until at last, by various
whispered compromises, the Georgians were persuaded to declare for independence without a silkworm clause specifically so worded, but with the addition of a more general clause stating that "He has refused his assent to laws, the most wholesome and necessary for the public good," which everyone agreed to

understand as referring to the silkworm crisis.

The day after that was consumed with fruitless wrangling: only Delaware held out, the two delegates still holding opposing opinions on independence. Thus, in fact, there was only one member left to be moved, but he was as immobile as the Alleghenies. It was finally decided that Mr. Rodney would have to be sent for to gain a clear majority one way or the other from Delaware. A rider was dispatched, with the hope that he would return with Mr. Rodney on the morrow.

In the evening we had supper with Dr. Franklin, who gave every evidence of being captivated by the charm of the divine Susanna. Indeed, I believe he must have given her some quite unmistakably clear evidence: for I had left the room to answer the call of nature, and when I returned Dr. Franklin was holding a wet rag over his eye. When I asked Susanna about it later, she would say only, "I accepted his apology."

Mr. Rodney arrived in due time, and spent the hour after his arrival excoriating the Congress in general and his brethren from Delaware in particular for making him ride all the way up to Philadelphia with the most appalling headache ever suffered by mortal man. It was some time before he ran out of breath; but at last Mr. Hancock was able to put the question to him directly.

"Independence, Mr. Rodney: Aye or nay?"

"Oh, yes, by all means, let us have independence, and let us all be hanged as traitors and put out of our misery," replied Mr. Rodney.

"Yes," Dr. Franklin began, "we must all hang together, or—"

"Shut up, Franklin," said Mr. Rodney, holding his

head in both hands.

"So finally the question is decided by Delaware," Mr. Wythe remarked.

"Which will doubtless be known for ever afterward as 'The Last State,' " added Mr. Harrison.

But at last the Congress was unanimous: we should have independence, if General Washington and his army could procure it for us. There remained yet some few clauses in the Declaration which did not please everyone, and another few days were expended in debating them. But in the end the document had been drawn up in a form that, if it did not please all the delegates, was at least no longer worth fighting over.

"Now, gentlemen," said Mr. Hancock on that memorable day, "what remains is for each of us to affix his signature to this Declaration, as a pledge that we shall all remain united in our determination to establish a permanent separation from the tyranny of King George."

"Yes," Dr. Franklin agreed, "we must all hang together, or we shall assuredly hang our heads in shame."

"That one needs some work before it goes in the almanac," said Mr. Clymer.

"Now, my friends," Mr. Hancock continued, "let there be no jealousy over the order of the signatures. We shall simply start on my right with the delegation from Georgia, and then we may go around the room in an orderly fashion."

"And if I may suggest," added Mr. Harrison, "we ought to leave a good space near the center for General Washington to sign at the next opportunity."

"Hear, hear," Mr. Chase concurred. "The General was a member of this Congress until we ourselves committed the command of the continental army to his care. He more than anyone else has brought us to the point where independency can be considered by reasonable men. Centuries from now, when the infant nation born this day has grown to a mighty empire of perhaps as many as eighteen or nineteen states, our distant progeny will treasure this Declaration and will look eagerly for the name of Washington subscribed to it."

Mr. Hancock looked a little sour, but all he said was, "Yes, of course; but first let us all sign it, so that the thing is finished and we are all pledged to independence."

"Yes," said Dr. Franklin, "for we must all hang loose, or we shall assuredly hang together."

"Keep working on it, Franklin," said Mr. Clymer.

Meanwhile the Georgian delegation had already subscribed, and then came the Carolinas, and so on from one end of the room to the other, until all but Mr. Hancock had signed.

"And now," said Mr. Samuel Adams, "it remains only for our President to add his name to the roll."

Mr. Hancock plunged the quill into the ink as if he meant it to soak up the whole pot.

"Don't forget to leave a space for—" Mr. John Adams began; but Mr. Hancock was already applying the quill to the Declaration with vigorous motions of his whole arm, extending all the way up into his shoulder.

"Why, Mr. Hancock," Mr. Gerry remarked after the President had lifted his hand from the paper with a final flourish, "you've left no room at all for General Washington's name!"

"Oops," said Mr. Hancock.

CHAPTER VII.

Washington's strategy on Long-Island.—A sudden marriage.—Escape to New-York by raft.—Attractions of New-York.—Mr. Hamilton's Drip-Down Economics.—Loss of New-York.—Crossing the Delaware.

BY the time we had left Philadelphia, Washington was on the move. He was heading for Long-Island, with the intention of preventing Howe from capturing the city of New-York. Susanna and I determined to meet him there in the town of Brooklyn, across the river from the city; and there we found him awaiting the arrival of Howe's force. The news of independence had, of course, reached him long before we did, and the soldiers were stirred by the idea that they were now fighting for something permanent.

"So what do you intend to do to prepare for Howe's arrival?" I asked him.

"Nothing," Washington responded confidently.

"Nothing?" Susanna and I both repeated at once.

"Precisely," said Washington. "You taught me that, Phillips. It worked for Forbes at Pittsburgh; it worked for us at Boston; it will work again here. Nothing, I might go so far as to say, is the greatest contribution our present age has made to the art of military strategy. In the future, wars will be fought entirely by armies doing nothing, nothing on a titanic scale; and think what a savings in men and material we shall have when opposing armies both adopt a strategy of doing nothing whatsoever! Furthermore, as doing nothing has been demonstrated to be the strategy that procures victory, both sides in future wars will invariably be victorious. There will be none of the bitterness of defeat and concomitant desire for revenge; but all men will live in amity in a world that is constantly at war, providing pleasant employment for young men in the armies and navies, and leaving the other classes of society to enjoy all the benefits of the profoundest peace. From now on, nothing is the strategy I intend to adopt."

Susanna was rubbing her temples as if suffering from a headache, but she apparently was resigned enough to hold her peace.

"Meanwhile," Washington continued, "I've set up my headquarters in this very commodious house, although I must say the ceilings are a bit low and the bed a bit short. I've set aside a room for you and Phillips to share, just upstairs and to the right, across from my own chamber."

"I'm sure I could find something in—"

"I won't hear of it," Washington said with finality. "After your journey you both must be in need of a good rest, and you'll find no accommodations but soldiers' tents elsewhere. I should like to have you with me and Parson Weems here, so please indulge me. Now, if you'll excuse me for a time, I have to make my usual rounds."

He left us alone in the house, and I immediately said to Susanna, "I can sleep in the parlor."

"It seems as if every man I meet tries to take advantage of my sex and my color," Susanna remarked.

"Except for you. You have always behaved as a gentleman to me."

"I've always tried to—"

"What is *wrong* with you?" she demanded with sudden vehemence.

"Susanna, I would never take advantage of a lady, in spite of all the pressing temptations I suffer every time you're near me—temptations I struggle mightily to resist, because I would not insult the finest lady I have ever known."

"And did you think you were the only one who was tempted?"

For a moment I stood mute and looked into her eyes. Then I asked carefully, "What do you mean, Susanna?"

"I mean, obviously, that I don't want you to sleep in the parlor."

"Then you really do feel...some attachment to me?"

"I have a weakness for perfect gentlemen."

I was probably gaping like a fish in a boat, because she continued:

"Mr. Gist, I know where I stand. I know I can never be more than a mistress to you. But even though—"

"By God, you're wrong!" I cried. "Susanna, I love you, and I know I can never deserve you, but if you're fool enough to have me, will you be my wife?"

A long interval of dreadful silence followed, until at last Susanna said quietly, "You're mad."

"I do believe I am. Since the moment I saw you a divine madness has taken possession of my soul, a madness that—"

"Oh, shut up!" Susanna exclaimed, and she enforced her will by pressing her lips hard against mine. She held them there until I had lost all desire to express my thoughts in articulate speech.

At last she spoke again: "I will be your wife, Mr. Gist, when we can do it, but I don't think I can wait that long."

"There's a clergyman in this very house," I reminded her.

"You mean that jackass?"

"A jackass with the power to make us both what we long to be." I took her hand and led her up the stairs, where we found Parson Weems sitting in his little room composing a tract.

"Weems," I said breathlessly, "marry us now."

Weems thought for a moment and then said, "Gist, may I have a brief word with you?"

"No," I replied. "Not without Susanna, who is bone of my bone and flesh of my flesh from this day forward."

"You do realize that I really am a clergyman, Gist, don't you? If I do this—"

"Weems, you fool! Do you think I'm plotting to seduce this lady with a sham marriage? By heaven, I should thrash you. But wedding now, and we'll save the thrashing for later."

"I'll do the wedding if you'll forgo the thrashing."

"Done," I said.

"Only do it quickly," Susanna added, clinging to me.

"All right," said Parson Weems. "Dearly beloved, et cetera, honorable estate and so on, skip to the good part. Do you, Susanna, take this man to be your lawfully wedded husband, for better for worse, for richer for poorer, whether he snores or not, till death do you part?"

"I do," she replied.

"And do you, Christopher, take this woman to be your lawfully wedded wife, under all the usual conditions et cetera?"

"I do," I answered eagerly.

"Then I now sentence you to be man and wife, and may God have mercy on your souls."

"We're done?" asked Susanna.

"For the rest of your natural lives," Weems replied.

Susanna yanked me out the door and into our own chamber, where what an hour before had been a dreadful temptation was now, by a few words spoken in front of the parson, mystically transformed into a sacred duty.

Our joy, though complete, was, however, short; for the next day Howe's army appeared, and it soon became evident that Washington's plan of doing absolutely nothing was not as effective as he had hoped. Howe had hemmed us in from both sides, and it was clear that, without something near a miracle, the army was lost.

But then the miracle came, and Susanna seized it. As evening came on, a thick fog settled in, and it was impossible to see more than a few paces in any direction.

"If only we had some way to slip across the river!" said Susanna. "We could be out of harm's way if we had boats, or even rafts."

"There are trees everywhere," I said.

"But it would be impossible to reduce them to logs quickly enough to do any good," Susanna responded.

"Are any of them cherry trees?" I asked.

"Oh!" said Parson Weems. "I see what you mean! There's a fine large stand of black cherries right by the river."

"Get us an axe," I told him, "and we'll go get Washington."

"I don't understand," said Susanna. "How is it easier to make logs from cherry trees?"

"You don't know Washington as well as we do, my love," I replied. Then I turned to find the nearest officer, who happened to be an old captain. "We need the men together and ready to build rafts. Any rope they can find, any fabric that can be twisted into ropes—have them gather as much as they can and go down to the river by the cherry grove. We'll provide the logs."

We found Washington eventually. It was difficult in the fog, but we kept asking soldiers until we found the place where he had fallen off his horse. We led him to the river, where the fog, by some providential dispensation, was dissipating; and when we came to the cherry trees, Washington did not need to be told what to do. The mania took hold of him before we said anything, and Susanna watched with awe as the trees were reduced to logs in a few minutes at most, with a terrifying din that must surely have been discouraging to the enemy. As soon as it was safe to approach, the soldiers began assembling the logs into rafts; and as the rafts were assembled, they set out for the lights across the river, where the fog had now entirely cleared.

By the next morning, the entire army had slipped out of Howe's grasp, and was safely lodged in New-

York, where the local militia supplemented our forces, and for the present Howe did not dare pursue us.

New-York in those days was a much smaller town than it is today; indeed, I believe there was scarcely a building over forty storeys in the whole island. But even in those days it was a town that loved a spectacle, and the movements of troops across the river, and the prospect of imminent invasion by Howe's army, did not prevent New-Yorkers from enjoying themselves.

Having disposed his troops as well as he could, Washington gave them a day's leave, and he himself spent the evening with Weems, Susanna, and me indulging in his favorite entertainment. He had learned that there was a popular puppet-show all the way up-town on Fourth-street; and, asking directions, was told to walk down the stairs at the next corner. These proved to lead down to an underground chamber hollowed out of a tunnel, where two dozen or so people were standing, apparently waiting for something. In a few minutes we heard the clopping of horses' hooves echoing in the tunnel, and a light was visible coming into the chamber. A team of eight horses entered, followed by a very long carriage; imitating the rest of the crowd, we entered the carriage, which was already stuffed with riders, so that we were forced to stand and cling to leathern straps hung from the ceiling, apparently for that purpose, as the carriage began to move and entered the dark tunnel once more.

Uncomfortable though the arrangements were, the carriage did convey us to Fourth-street, which, when we emerged from the subterranean conveyance, proved to be lined with theaters and expositions of every sort. We found the puppet-show, where we enjoyed the amusing adventures of a cast of oddly shaped befurred puppets with bulging white eyes—most of the audience laughing in delight, but Washington watching with his usual stony dignity and expressionless silence.

After the show, Parson Weems, Susanna, and I retreated to a popular tavern across the street for a bit of Madeira; but Washington's eye was attracted by a poster advertising an exhibition in the rooms next to the tavern:

THE INCOMPARABLE DERWIN

AND

THE INCOMPARABLE SHERWIN

TWIN BROTHERS WHO ARE

INCOMPARABLY DIFFERENT,

ONE FROM ANOTHER

He told us he would meet us in the tavern, and went in to enjoy the exhibition. Some time later he joined us, and declared himself well pleased with what he had seen. "It really is remarkably interesting," he said. "The men are twins, and yet you cannot imagine two men more different in every respect."

"How did you know they were twins?" asked Parson Weems.

Washington looked surprised and shocked. "I took it upon their word as gentlemen."

The rest of us decided not to pursue that line of inquiry. Instead, I turned the conversation to the question of what was to be done now that Howe occupied Long island and was doubtless plotting to move on New-York itself.

"Nothing," Washington replied with confidence.

"Nothing?" Susanna repeated incredulously. "But surely what happened across the river must have persuaded you that it is necessary to do *something!*"

"What happened there, I am quite convinced, was entirely owing to the malevolent influence of Irving. It was not the strategy that was at fault, but merely the events."

"But—" Susanna began, and then stopped and took a very big gulp of her Madeira.

"To my mind," said Parson Weems, "our most pressing problem is one of money. The soldiers have not been paid for some time. If they are not paid soon, they will begin to desert."

"They had better not," Washington replied with some warmth. "I am not a cruel man, but I do believe in strong discipline, and if I have to send men to bed without supper, I will do it."

"I must agree with the Parson," I said. "Even the sternest discipline will not keep the men long if we cannot pay them what they are legitimately owed. We must find a way to persuade the Congress to deal with the question of paying the army."

"And I'm sure the Congress will respond with alacrity once we have made our case," said Washington. "Meanwhile, I have been thinking of erecting a fort at the northern end of the island."

"A very good idea, General," said Susanna, obviously pleased. "If we control the navigation up the Hudson, we deprive the enemy of the opportunity to drive a wedge between the East and the Middle."

"True," said Washington. "I had not thought of that. I was more interested in establishing the site of a new city on Manhattan Island—a city that, as it grows, will doubtless eclipse New-York to the south, and perhaps even absorb it; a city that will soon rival even Philadelphia as a center of our new American civilization; a city called Washington. A fort, of course, will be the seed from which such a city sprouts. And there is one more thing I've been think-ing of, Phillips."

"What is that, General?"

"You're a lieutenant, aren't you?"

"Yes, sir."

"Would you mind terribly being a captain?"

She glanced at me, and then answered, "No, sir."

"Good. Captain Phillips it is, then."

Susanna smiled broadly. "Thank you, sir."

"You are, after all, the architect of the nothing strategy, and you deserve recognition. Perhaps in the future nothing will be named for you."

Susanna's smile froze on her face as she repeated, "Thank you, sir."

Washington found us lodgings in a rather large inn. Susanna and I had a room on the twenty-seventh floor, which required a bit of labor in climbing the stairs, but rewarded us with a fine view of the city. I told Susanna I was very proud to be married to the most beautiful captain in the continental army, and we spent a very pleasant night together. It would be the last pleasant night for some time.

In the morning, when we found Washington (rather late, since Susanna and I had slept but little), he was in earnest discussion with a small, energetic man who seemed to be explaining something to him, while writing or drawing something on a paper in front of him.

"Ah! Gist—Phillips—just the men I wanted to see," Washington said when he saw us. "This is Mr. Alexander Hamilton, a young fellow who has the most amazing ideas about money. Mr. Hamilton, this is Mr. Gist, my trusted advisor; and the other young man is Captain Phillips, one of my most valuable officers."

The small man named Hamilton looked perplexed. "Other young man?" he repeated.

"The one in the uniform, of course."

Hamilton continued to look perplexed for a moment, and then appeared to decide that perplexity was not worth the effort. "Very pleased to meet you both, uh, gentlemen."

"Mr. Hamilton was just explaining to me how to get all the money we need for the army," Washington continued. "It turns out that the Congress can have all the money it wants by simply increasing military spending and lowering taxes."

"Don't you mean raising taxes?" Susanna asked.

"Ah! That's the clever part," Washington replied. "Explain it to them, Hamilton."

Mr. Hamilton turned his paper over to its blank side and started drawing something while he spoke. "You see, military spending stimulates economic activity by creating demand for manufactured products. But higher taxes have the opposite effect by reducing the incentive to get rich. By lowering taxes, we create incentive to gain wealth, and the wealth is then spent on luxury items, creating more wealth for the producers thereof, and thus raising tax revenue overall."

I looked at the paper in front of him. He had drawn a sort of crude outline of a bell.

"And is this drawing some sort of graphic representation of your theory?" I asked.

"No. That's just a drawing of the Liberty Bell. Sorry—I always doodle like that when I'm explaining things. It's a nervous habit."

"It seems to me," said Susanna, "that the incentive to get rich is that, once you've done it, you're rich. Even if you take away fifty per cent, if I make a thousand pounds, I still get to keep five hundred, so I'm five hundred pounds better off."

Hamilton gave her a condescending smile. "I don't expect military... uh, men to understand economics."

"I'm sending Hamilton down to Philadelphia to explain all this to the Congress," said Washington. "All they have to do is lower taxes and spend more money on the army, and everything will be fine."

"Do you really think the Congress will be that..." Susanna searched for an appropriate adjective, and at last came up with "...amenable?"

"Oh," replied Washington, "the Congress is—heh— the Congress—heh heh heh—best minds of the—ha ha ha ha ha—of the—ha ha ha ha ha!"

The laughing fit was now fully upon him, and Washington was pounding his great fists on the table, nearly upsetting the inkpot, trying to speak but finding it impossible.

"It is the effect of a puppet-show he saw last night," I explained to poor Hamilton, who was watching with an expression of barely suppressed terror.

Washington threw his head back and exclaimed, "The blue one lives in a garbage can!" Then he fell forward, banging his forehead repeatedly on the table, so that the ink spilled all over Mr. Hamilton's bell.

It was some time before he recovered. But eventually Mr. Hamilton was sent off to Philadelphia to persuade the Congress, and I wished him very good luck with that.

Meanwhile, things did not go well in New-York, and Washington's strategy of doing nothing did not bear the fruit he had hoped it would bear. Even as Hamilton set off for Philadelphia, Howe, reinforced by Hessian mercenaries, invaded New-York, and our brave soldiers ran all the way across New-Jersey before they stopped. Washington eventually regrouped what was left of his army west of the Delaware, but that was not very much, most of the soldiers having deserted along the way.

All was not lost, however: two or three days after we arrived on the west bank of the Delaware, Susanna, Parson Weems, and I were very much surprised to see that little Hamilton fellow walking toward us.

"Mr. Hamilton!" I greeted him. "What a surprise to see you here! How did your mission to the Congress go?"

"Perfectly, of course," he said, with the air of one confident that all his projects must always proceed perfectly. "I explained my 'Drip-Down Theory' to the Congress, which sent me back with the entire back pay of the army in specie."

"So at last the soldiers can be paid," Parson Weems said. "I'm sure that will come as very good news to the ones who are left. Where is the money?"

"I left it with General Washington," replied Hamilton. "He's down by the river in that direction."

Weems was the first to give voice to the sudden fear that had gripped me as well. "You mean you left the General with a bag of coins? Beside a river? Alone?"

"Was that unwise?" asked Hamilton.

We said nothing; we simply began running toward the river. Susanna followed, and Hamilton trailed behind us, saying,

"Surely you don't mean to imply that the General can't be trusted!"

But we merely kept running for the river, whither we arrived just in time to see Washington, surrounded by empty sacks, hurling one of of the dollars the Congress had provided across the Delaware.

"What is he doing?" Susanna asked in disbelief.

"He can't help himself," I said to her; then to Washington, "Washington! For heaven's sake, stop!"

"I have to stop anyway," he said cheerfully. "I ran out of dollars."

"But, general," cried Susanna, "that money was all we had to pay the soldiers!"

"Was it? I suppose it was. I didn't think of that. I saw dollars, and I saw a river, and the rest just naturally followed. My word! It felt good. I haven't done that in a very long time."

"But *why?*" Susanna demanded.

"I don't think I understand the question," Washington replied.

"And how will you get the dollars back?" Parson Weems asked in a mildly disapproving tone.

"By the usual method, I suppose. We'll cross the river and retrieve them."

"But the other side of the river is crawling with

Hessians," Weems reminded him.

"Oh—is it? I suppose it is."

Nevertheless, there was nothing else to be done. The men had to be paid, or we should have no more army. The money was on the other side of the river. We found a few boats nearby and decided to send a small patrol across to retrieve the money if it could be done. I recommended that some subordinate officer be found to lead the patrol, but Washington would not hear of it. I therefore placed myself in Washington's boat, with Susanna (over my objections) beside me, and we set out across the icy Delaware, fully expecting (at least for my own part) to be shot before we even reached the opposite shore.

No shots were fired, however, and when we reached the other side it became apparent why that was so. Bodies of Hessian soldiers were strewn all over the ground. At first I wondered whether some local militia had come before us and massacred the men; but as we came closer it became clear that the Hessian soldiers were not dead, but unconscious, lying in a field of Spanish milled dollars. The hail of coins had been too much for them, and each dollar hurled by the mighty arm of Washington had found its target on a Hessian skull.

"Well," said Washington, "this is very convenient. Disarm these men and take them prisoner, and we can collect our money and our prisoners and take them back with us."

"Or," said Susanna, "we can bring the rest of the army across and press forward and take Trenton."

"Would that be good?" asked Washington.

"Very good," I told him. "The Hessian troops lie

here, our prisoners. Trenton is undefended, and Trenton is the capital of the province."

"Oh! Well, in that case, by all means. Excellent thinking, Phillips."

Thus, having crossed the Delaware, Washington was able, by a singular stroke of good fortune, to take Trenton. The cause of independence, which had seemed so nearly hopeless after the loss of New-York, was once again embraced by public opinion.

CHAPTER VIII.

Difficulties maintaining the army.—Philadelphia lost; Congress removes to York.—Mr. Hamilton's plan for a new form of money.—Disappointing results in first trial of Hamilton's money.—A visit to Ferry Farm.—Washington's lost treasure.

THE campaign in New-Jersey was a resounding success for Washington, but the success was not as lasting as we had hoped. At first, indeed, its effects were nearly miraculous. Our struggling army was reinforced by thousands of new recruits who were keen to serve under the great Washington, who, being now just an inch short of eight feet tall, more truly deserved the epithet "great" than any other general of his era. But with the new recruits came the difficult problem of paying them, a problem that would haunt us for some time until Washington himself hit on an ingenious solution, as will be narrated in its proper place. The discipline of the army was chronically lax as well, for most of the officers were themselves new recruits, and they refused to adopt such extreme measures as sending men to bed without supper, or, what they dreaded most, making them write "I will not desert the continental army" one hundred times, a punishment Washington reserved for repeat offenders.

Meanwhile Howe was not inactive. New-York being securely occupied, Howe was able to land an enormous army just below Philadelphia. Washington attempted to oppose Howe in a straightforward manner, but while he was giving Howe an honest and straightforward battle, and not without some success, Lord Cornwallis marched deviously around to our right flank and surprised us, which Washington regarded as simple cheating. The result, which even to this day I blush to relate, was that we lost Philadelphia. The Congress managed to escape just before Howe's army marched into the city, and removed to York, where some of the members indulged a simmering resentment against Washington. Our army settled in at Valley Forge, and there we spent a miserable winter, in which, however, some of the qualities of true greatness manifested themselves in the General.

One afternoon Washington was in an unusually cheerful state as he came back to his headquarters after his daily rounds in the camp. Susanna and I, along with Parson Weems, were put up in the house with Washington (a luxury that gave me occasional pangs of guilt when I thought of the soldiers in their icy tents), so we were sitting by the fire when Washington came in with Hamilton in tow and announced that the pay problem was solved.

"That's very good news indeed," I said. "How did we get the money?"

"Oh, we haven't got it yet. But Hamilton has figured out a way to get the money from the Congress."

"I thought," said Susanna, "that the last time we asked for money, the Congress replied that, owing to Mr. Hamilton's program of spending more and taxing less, all they could come up with was two shillings, four pence, and three brass buttons."

"Yes,' replied Washington, "but the beauty of Mr. Hamilton's new plan is that the Congress need not actually have the money to give it to us."

"You mean they'll steal it from somebody else?" asked Susanna.

"Of course not. Explain it to them, Hamilton."

"My thought," Hamilton explained, "is that we can simply instruct the Congress to have the money we need printed."

"Printed?" I think Weems, Susanna, and I all repeated the word together.

"Precisely. You see the beauty of it, don't you? Instead of coins, the soldiers will simply receive small slips of paper with the words 'One Dollar,' 'Five Dollars,' 'Ten Dollars,' or what have you, printed on them, and will use them the same way they would use coins in the same denominations."

"But why would they think a piece of paper was worth ten dollars?" Weems asked.

"Why do we think a piece of gold is worth ten dollars?" Hamilton returned.

"Well, because," Weems began, "because it's—well, because it's gold."

"Precisely," said Hamilton. "We think gold is valuable because we agree to think gold is valuable. Why? We cannot eat gold; we cannot build shelter with it; we cannot burn it to keep ourselves warm. We can only exchange it for the things we really need, because we agree that a very small quantity of gold is worth a very large quantity of food. Its value depends entirely on our agreement: it is not in any way intrinsic. Now, my very simple plan is this: that, in the same way we have agreed to regard gold as valuable, so we shall now agree to regard money on paper as valuable. Once again, our simple agreement will suffice to create the value."

"Isn't it a remarkable thought?" asked Washington.

"Remarkable," Susanna agreed, although her tone suggested that there was room for more than one kind of remark on the subject.

"I'm sending Hamilton to York to speak to the Congress about it," said Washington. "Just imagine—in our new North American empire, no one need ever be poor again. We can provide all the money every citizen of these United States will ever need for any purpose whatsoever.—Come along, Hamilton: I'll write a letter for you to take with you detailing the successes of our current campaign; for I trust, sir, that you understand the value of a good dispatch."

With those words, Washington led Hamilton into the back room he used as his office.

"One of them is an imbecile and the other one is mad," Parson Weems remarked.

"It seems to me," said Susanna, "that there is no reason why they could not both be imbeciles."

I must own that I had not expected much result from Hamilton's expedition, but a few weeks later he was back with stacks of freshly printed money, which was distributed forthwith to the puzzled soldiers. I say "puzzled," though in many cases "mutinous" might have been a more nearly accurate description.

Hamilton, however, was full of optimism; and Susanna and I went with him to demonstrate the utility of his new form of money by using it to buy some sorely needed potatoes from a nearby farm.

"Dollar a bushel," the farmer replied when asked the price of his potatoes. I might have spent some time negotiating with the man, but Hamilton was eager to present his new creation, and therefore simply asked for ten bushels, and handed the man a ten-dollar note.

"What's this?" the farmer asked.

"It's ten dollars," replied Hamilton.

"No it isn't," said the farmer. "It's a piece of paper that says 'Ten Dollars' on it."

"But it is in fact ten dollars," Hamilton told him. "You see here where it says, 'By act of Congress, this note is legal tender for all debts, public and private.' "

"I don't need a tender," the farmer insisted. "I need ten dollars."

"Precisely," said Hamilton, undaunted. "I'm giving you this piece of paper with 'Ten Dollars' printed on it. And because we agree that it is worth ten dollars, it is in fact worth ten dollars."

"Tell you what," said the farmer. "You give me that piece of paper with 'Ten Dollars' written on it, and I'll give you a piece of paper with 'Ten Bushels of Potatoes' written on it."

"But a piece of paper won't feed the men," Hamilton objected.

"It will if they agree that it is in fact ten bushels of potatoes," the farmer replied. "Won't it?"

In the end we did not succeed in procuring our ten bushels of potatoes, and for the most part the men were similarly unsuccessful in exchanging their paper money for useful goods. Hamilton himself refused to be entirely discouraged, but the men were cold and hungry. To make matters worse, not only could we not persuade the

Congress to do anything for us, but in fact we could not even find the Congress. Fearing a surprise attack, the men of the Congress had turned peripatetic. From York they moved to Lancaster, and then to Annapolis, and then to Baltimore, to Winchester, to Cumberland, to Pittsburgh, and briefly (owing to the gentlemen's refusal to stop and ask directions) to Mexico City. We were left to our own devices, and it seemed as though we should eventually lose our army altogether without some means of procuring money in the form of coins rather than paper.

"Of course there is much to be hoped for from the French," said Washington when we were discussing the situation one bitter morning in late winter. "I have every confidence in our diplomats. Dr. Franklin reports that the French women are particularly susceptible. I have no doubt that he has spent every evening explaining to the court ladies that it is to France's advantage to have a strong American empire that is well disposed toward France and capable of defending their remaining North American interests.

"You mean St.-Pierre and Miquelon?" asked Parson Weems.

"Exactly. Surely the French will see the wisdom of balancing British power in the north with a great independent empire to the south."

"The French may or may not come to our aid," said Susanna, "but for the present we need money. We need to be candid and admit to ourselves that the paper-money project has been a failure."

"The fault is not on our side," Hamilton insisted. "We have maintained from the beginning that the money is in fact worth exactly the value printed on it. It is the ill-bred and uneducated bumpkins who inhabit these parts who are to blame: they refuse to see the logic of the notion, and to be absolutely frank I suspect them of Tory sympathies."

"At the moment we must be practical," I said. "For reasons we may or may not know, our suppliers refuse to accept our paper money, whereas we know they would accept money in specie. It is vital to our cause that we obtain money they will accept. Can anyone think of any possibilities?"

"I think we've run out of possibilities," Weems remarked grimly.

"Gentlemen," said Washington, "we certainly cannot allow ourselves to lose hope: for, as the old proverb has it,—" (he brought out the tattered copybook, and we waited patiently for him to find his page)—" 'Do not chew your nails in the sight of others.' The wisdom of our fathers, gentlemen, when understood metaphorically, is an ever-present help in managing our affairs. For my own part, I am convinced that our current difficulties all spring from the evil machinations of Irving, and I refuse to give him the satisfaction of letting him see me despair."

"Irving?" asked Hamilton.

"The wicked invisible mule who bedevils him throughout his life," Weems explained.

Hamilton looked helpless: his question had been answered, but not in a way that satisfied him intellectually.

"I cannot believe," said Susanna, "that there are no possibilities left to us."

"In fact I *can* think of *one* possibility," Washington said.

"What's that?" asked Weems. "And don't tell me it

involves any more invisible livestock."

"When I was a boy, I used to spend hours at Ferry Farm throwing Spanish milled dollars across the Rappahannock. It became, as you know, a lifelong habit, but I have never since had so much leisure to indulge in the sport. There were times when I went to the riverbank day after day to spend all afternoon throwing dollars. That was how I developed the accuracy for which, I may say without boasting, I am still noted."

"And how will that help us right now?" I asked.

"Well, I never brought any of them back."

We looked at him in stunned silence.

"There were always more, you see. We seem to have had a good many Spanish milled dollars. It was never necessary to retrieve them, because there were always more to throw."

"Do you mean you think that, in all these years, no one has picked up the dollars you threw across the Rappahannock?" Susanna asked, trying not to sound too incredulous.

"The other side of the river is Washington land, too. Why would anyone be looking for dollars there?"

"So you mean," I said, "that if we went down there right now, we'd find some of the money you threw?"

"It's worth trying," said Washington. "Gist, why don't you head down there now? See what you can find, and then we'll have something to pay the soldiers."

It sounded very dubious to me. "Well, I'm, uh, not sure—"

"Take Phillips with you. You may need more than one man to carry the money back."

"I'm, uh, not—"

"We'll go right away, General," Susanna declared.

Why was Susanna suddenly interested in this unlikely prospect? I had learned not to discount any idea of hers, but it did not seem reasonable to expect that Washington's idly flung dollars should still be waiting for him after so many years.

"I think we should take Mr. Hamilton with us as well," Susanna added. And now I was certain she had some notion in her mind, but what it was I could not guess. When Washington seemed to hesitate, she added, "He's very good at finding money."

"That is true. Very well then," Washington agreed. "Take Hamilton with you, find the dollars, and you should have enough to pay the soldiers, with a little left over for Madeira. Best set off at once: for, as they say" (and here he produced his copybook, and we waited for him to find the appropriate citation): " 'If others talk at dinner, be attentive, but do not speak with your mouth full.' "

We had to go by land, as the British made the sea route unreliable. Susanna has always been an excellent rider. I at least can stay on the horse, and Hamilton was not entirely hopeless; our progress, therefore was fairly rapid.

At our first stop, Hamilton took the opportunity to ask the obvious questions about Susanna.

"She is my wife," I explained in a tone that I hoped would answer all unexpressed questions.

But Hamilton persisted.

"Why, then, is she also a man called Phillips?"

Susanna replied, "We find it best not to contradict the general too often. It confuses him."

"Is that why we've come looking for lost treasure?" Hamilton asked. "Are we making a useless journey of several days and unknown dangers because no one wants to contradict General Washington?"

"No," Susanna replied, and I listened attentively myself to hear her explanation. "Your mission to the Congress showed that you have an aptitude for parting rich fools from their money. Virginia is stuffed with rich fools, and such a man as you ought to be able to extract enough from them for our purposes."

"But what shall I tell them?"

"Just draw another picture of the Liberty Bell," Susanna replied, "and tell them the same nonsense you told us."

Hamilton was not convinced that the same nonsense would apply, and was worried that he might have to come up with different nonsense in order to persuade the Virginia planters to come up with the back pay of an entire army. Nevertheless, in broad outline, Susanna's plan seemed a reasonable one.

We agreed, however, that it would be necessary at least to pay a quick visit to Ferry Farm, so as to be able to assure the General (for he himself was so naturally honest that we should have been ashamed to lie to him) that we had done our best to retrieve his long-lost dollars. Accordingly we found the old plantation, which had, by various curiosities of wills and inheritance laws, passed into the hands of Washington's elderly Uncle Cedric, who answered the door and received out awkward greetings.

"Little Georgie," he said when we had told him of our errand. "How many years have passed since I saw him! Is he out of short pants yet?"

"I can assure you that his pants are quite long," I replied. "In fact he is general of the continental army."

"Always loved to play soldiers, our little Georgie, especially when his father took away his hatchet. He needs money, you say? I might be able to find a few shillings in my coat pocket."

"We thought we might borrow your boat, if you would be so kind," Susanna said. "General Washington suggested there might be a few coins across the river."

"Might be. Or pine cones. If you can use pine cones, I'm sure it's the place to look."

Susanna thanked him and headed toward the shore; I was beginning to follow her when Uncle Cedric took my arm and said in a confidential undertone, "That young man" (pointing to Susanna)—"does it strike you that there's something odd about him?"

"Well,..." I began hesitantly.

"I think he looks pale," said Uncle Cedric. "I hope he's not ill."

I assured him that I would look after the pale young man, and then Hamilton and I joined her at the boat. Before I could say anything, Susanna took the oars, which I suppose was her prerogative as the only military man among us, and with energetic strokes she took us across the Rappahannock in good time.

The other side of the river was a forest of tall pines, and our footsteps seemed preternaturally silent in the thick carpet of needles that made the ground a rich uniform sable color.

"Nothing but pine needles and a few cones," Hamilton remarked, and his voice was jarringly loud in the silence of the winter forest.

I looked around, idly scraping my foot through the needles. "I'm afraid you're right, But at least we can tell the General—"

"Look!" cried Susanna, pointing toward my feet.

I looked down. Where I had scraped the ground, something metallic was glinting through the needles. Quickly I stooped and started brushing away the needles with my hands. Under them was a layer on the ground made up entirely of Spanish milled dollars.

Susanna knelt down where she stood and swept away the needles, and there, too, she found a carpet of dollars.

I stood and took half a dozen strides and stooped again. And Susanna did the same, and Hamilton joined us; and for quite some time wherever we brushed away the needles, we found a uniform layer of dollars below. It took us at least half an hour to delineate the limits of the field of dollars, and most of it was done by Susanna and me, for a strange lassitude had overcome Hamilton. He lay on his back, his fingers slowly gripping and releasing the coins beneath him.

"Are you feeling ill, Mr. Hamilton?" Susanna finally asked him.

"I want to live here," replied Hamilton. "No—I want to die here. Nothing will ever equal this. My life has reached its peak, and no experience will ever bring joy to me again. I have lived as much as I care to live, and it would be fitting now that I should be taken directly to the heavenly Jerusalem, which is the only greater joy I can ever hope to experience."

"Mr. Hamilton," said Susanna, "you are still a

young man, and life has many joys waiting for you. You will find love, and—"

"I *have* found love, Captain, uh, Phillips! I am passionately in love with money, money in all its forms, beautiful gold, ravishing silver, charming copper, neatly printed slips of paper;—I desire money as other men desire their mistresses! And here is a forest made of money! If you were suddenly placed among the seventy-two willing virgins of the Mohammedan heaven, would you have any desire to leave that spot? Well, not you personally, captain—forgive me—the uniform, you see, makes me forget the lady—but I have found my seventy-two virgins! I have found the earthly paradise, and now it must be broken up and taken away. I must be cast out of Eden, and cherubim with a flaming sword must keep me from the tree of life. What reason have I to live any longer?"

"We are founding a new government," said Susanna, "with all the problems of government to be solved—including the question of money."

"Yes," I added, "you will be present at the birth of a new pecuniary system. Is that not something to live for?"

He sat up with a start. "A new *kind* of money?"

"Yes, Mr. Hamilton," said Susanna. "The coin of the United States of America."

"Why, yes! That *is* true," said Hamilton. "It will be only fitting that I should be present at the birth of an entirely new species of specie. How many true lovers of money are afforded that opportunity?"

"But first," Susanna continued, "we must win the war, and to do that we must pay the army."

This argument was enough to bring Hamilton out of

his lethargy; and, with a last wistful look at the forest of dollars, he began helping us gather the coins into large piles. Then he and Susanna went back to find a large number of sacks, while I sat in the silent forest to guard the piles of coins from no one except a ragged-looking fish crow, which took enough of an interest in the shiny dollars to make it worth my while to chase the bird away.

It took many trips with the boat to bring the hoard across the river, and then we had to arrange for what amounted to a caravan to transport it all back to Pennsylvania; but of course we had all the funds we could possibly need to pay for the wagons, drivers, and escorts. We finally reached Valley Forge in the spring—only to find an enormous army marching in just as we arrived.

At first all of us presumed the worst; but then we spotted the fleur-de-lis flag and realized that the French had arrived at last, and in numbers we had not dared hope for.

Just as we reached Washington with the good news that we had found his trove of dollars, the French commander made his appearance.

"La Fayette, I am here, yes?" he announced. "Which one is the général Washington?"

CHAPTER IX.

Washington and La Fayette meet.—They compare invisible animals.—Colonel de Trop reappears.—Baron von Steuben disciplines our army.—Washington's tale of the three wine merchants, the innkeeper, the lady with the carbuncle pendant, the cursed sailor, the talking monkey, the ruined temple, and the cask of the best wine in the world.

"Général Washington, sir!—the hero of the American independence! I have great honor to meet you at last!"

"The honor is mine, General Fayette. I have heard much of your accomplishments in France."

"Have you truly?" asked General La Fayette.

"Well, no. But I thought it would be a thing to say. Did it not sound well? We have arranged for you to make your headquarters in a small house nearby; not a palace, but commodious in its way."

"Your consideration is very appreciated," said La Fayette. "But tell me—is it that you have heard a sound, which one might describe as 'yapping'?"

"Yapping? No, I don't believe so."

"Ah! It is good. I have fear that Sophie might have followed me from the France. One must be careful, you know."

"A lady friend?" asked Washington.

"No! Sophie, she is caniche, yes? Poodle. My mortal

enemy, though one sees her not."

"And she lives to deepen your sorrows, to blast your victories, and to hound you to an early grave?"

"Yes! By blue, Washington, how is it that you knew?"

"My word, Fayette! I knew you were a great general the moment I saw you. All great military commanders (as I learned, sir, from one of the greatest of them all) are pursued throughout their careers by the forces of envy and malice, personified in malevolent invisible animals. I myself have been relentlessly dogged by the mule Irving." Washington stooped down and shook General La Fayette's hand warmly, and from that moment the two were the best of friends.

And then there appeared another officer from the clot of French soldiers, and it seemed that were was something familiar about him. But it was Washington who recognized him first.

"Lieutenant de Trop!" he called out in delight.

"It's Colonel de Trop now," the officer replied with a smile. "And my heavens, you *are* the same Washington I met at Fort Le Boeuf! But I believe you have grown somewhat taller."

"I may have done, Colonel, but I have not outgrown my gratitude to you. You remember Mr. Gist, of course."

I shook the colonel's hand and exchanged polite greetings with him. Much later, when Washington and La Fayette had gone off together, I asked the colonel, "Is your name really de Trop?"

"General Washington," he replied, "is a hero to every true Frenchman, and my name, sir, is whatever he wants it to be. And who is this very charming officer?" he asked, turning to Susanna.

"My wife Susanna," I replied. "Susanna, this is Colonel, uh, de Trop, who was very courteous to us when Washington and I visited Fort Le Boeuf years ago."

"Very pleased to meet you, sir," Susanna said, offering her hand.

Instead of shaking her hand, the colonel raised it to his lips and kissed it. "Upon my faith, Mr. Gist, I should never have believed it if one had told it to me, but you Americans have made an improvement in gallantry of which we French had not even dreamed. What man would not beg to join your army if he might serve under such delightful officers?"

"Susanna is...unique," I said.

"General Washington believes I am a man named Phillips," Susanna explained. "And, as you say, my name is whatever he wants it to be."

"And why, if I may be forgiven for asking, did you come into the army in the first place?" the colonel asked.

"It seemed to me, sir, that the military life would afford me more opportunities for indulging in my favorite pastime."

"What is that, dear lady?" the colonel asked with a smile.

"Killing Redcoats," she replied with a sweet smile of her own.

Before the colonel could make any answer to that, a loud voice came from behind him, rapidly approaching: "Mine God! This is what they an army call? It is not possible!"

"Oh," said the colonel. "Mr. Gist, and, uh, Captain Phillips, this is a friend of General La Fayette's, Baron von Steuben. Baron von Steuben, Captain Phillips and Mr. Gist."

Ignoring the introduction, the Baron continued, "No uniforms of which to speak of, tents will he und also nill he distributed, no military exercises I see anywhere—this is the most ragged und tagged mess which I ever have seen! Und look you—negresses for officers!"

Susanna's right hand was involuntarily closing into a fist. I gave her a warning glance, which was like giving a gentle word of admonition to an earthquake.

Fortunately Colonel de Trop intervened, desperately working to keep the conversation pleasant. "Baron von Steuben is a Prussian, and a great believer in military discipline."

"Until today!" the Baron barked. "Now, mine God! I know not. Believe I even that military discipline exists? But yes, if my way I have, your American army disciplined shall be!"

"Oh," I said. "Well...thank you."

"Good luck," Susanna added quietly.

In the morning Washington, Susanna, and I rose early and walked over to La Fayette's headquarters, where we found him busy nailing a brass plaque to the door, a plaque on which was engraved,

ICI DORMIT LE MARQUIS DE LA FAYETTE

"Ah! Washington, my friend!" he said as he continued hammering. "You will forgive me for completing this task, but I wished to lose no time. Gratitude is like the concombre, yes?”

“I know precisely what you mean!” Washington exclaimed in delight. “Ah, Fayette, we shall get along famously.”

Meanwhile Baron von Steuben had gone around the camp and roused a large number of sergeants at dawn, and was now drilling them in an open field, shouting insults that they only half-comprehended.

“That will not end well for Steuben,” Susanna remarked.

I told her to give the man a chance.

“I *am* giving him a chance,” she replied. “I am giving him a chance to get a blackened eye from them instead of me.”

Later, as we were pulling Baron von Steuben out of the barrel of sauerkraut into which he had been thrust upside-down, Parson Weems suggested a small wager: which would kill the Baron first—the enlisted men or Susanna? I told him I did not believe in gambling, at which he reminded me that he wore the collar, not I. I in turn reminded him that Steuben would also have me to deal with if he offered any insult to Susanna, and therefore his wager did not take all the possibilities into account; but Weems replied, “No, Gist; for we both know, begging your pardon, that no insult to Susanna goes unavenged long enough for you to intervene.” To all this the Baron said nothing; but as soon as he was cleaned up, he was out drilling some enlisted men again, which I thought showed admirable patience.

Our supper that evening was delayed until Baron von Steuben had cleaned himself up after being pulled out of the latrine; but once we were all seated, we ate better than we had done in quite some time. The French had brought not only soldiers, but money as well, and it was remarkable how quickly supplies appeared for sale when it was known that there were golden louis to be had, as well as the Spanish milled dollars we had brought from Virginia. La Fayette, whose disposition was naturally generous, made sure the American soldiers ate as well as the French did. Cries of "Long live Fayette!" could be heard all over the camp. I was glad to see the men so happy, and I was also glad to share in the excellent claret which La Fayette had brought with him. Washington made sure, for his part, to bring out his finest Madeira. Soon a friendly dispute arose, with La Fayette contending for the superiority of French claret, and Washington taking the part of Madeira, while Steuben advanced the claims of the hock from the valley of the Moselle. After much discussion among the three of them, Washington proposed a toast to "Germany, France, and Madeira, which have labored so fruitfully to give us pleasure." And then he continued:

"If it will not offend you, gentlemen, I should like to tell you a story, which was related to me by my late brother Lawrence; for it has no little bearing on the matter under discussion. Once, so it is said, there were three merchants: a seller of hock, a seller of claret, and a seller of Madeira; and as they traveled they happened to meet along the road. As their businesses were so similar, they naturally conceived friendly feelings one for another; and when evening came, they stopped together at the same inn.

"In this inn, they naturally fell to discussing the relative merits of their merchandise; and the innkeeper overhearing their conversation, that worthy gentle-man approached them, saying, 'Sirs, I have heard your dispute over which wine is the best, and I would have you know, gentlemen, that it is a question to which I alone possess the answer; for in that cask in the corner of the room, sirs, is the best wine in the world.'

" 'By all means,' said the claret merchant, 'let us try a sample of this wine; if it is truly the best in the world, we will not stick at the price.'

" 'I may not open the cask,' the innkeeper replied, 'for I have given my solemn word; nor have I ever tasted the wine myself.'

" 'But, good heavens, man, how can you say it is the best wine in the world,' asked the merchant of Madeira, 'if you have never even tasted it?'

" 'Ah,' said the innkeeper, 'it is because of the circumstances under which I received the cask; and when I have once narrated them to you, I am so certain that you will agree that this is the best wine in the world, that I will wager you your night's accommodations on it. These circumstances, sirs, I will now relate.

" 'When I was some years younger, my father left me this inn, which to speak in very truth was not so much of an inheritance; for it was not as much frequented in those days, and many nights would pass when nary a traveler appeared. It was on one of those nights, when I had gone to bed already—for it was a night of intermittent but ferocious storms, and such a night as no wise traveler would choose for his journey, —it was on such a night, I say, that I was awakened by a pounding on the front door. Dressing hastily, I took a candle in my hand and descended the stairs, where the pounding still continued. As soon as I opened the door, a hooded figure dashed in past me and took a position in the parlor by the last dying embers of the fire. I closed the door and followed; but you may well imagine my surprise when the hood was thrown back to reveal the most beautiful face I have ever beheld in my life. It was a young woman, no more than one-and-twenty, with an ivory complexion brought into relief by cheeks flushed with carmine, and a cascade of loose hair as red as flame.

" ' "Madam," said I, "how may I be of assistance?"

" ' "If you would be so good as to start the fire again, I should be most grateful," she replied; "and then, sir, I have great need of a worthy man to whom I can entrust the priceless treasure that sits on the wagon outside."

" ' "If it be within my power to assist you," I assured her, "you shall be assisted."

" ' "But I must first determine whether it *is* in your power," said she. "When you have made the fire, I shall tell you my conditions."

" 'It was the work of a moment to lay more logs and kindling on the fire and fan it into a roaring flame. As soon as the heat filled the room, the lady let her cloak fall; and if my eyes had been ravished before, you may be sure that I could barely speak now: for the lady was dressed, not for traveling, but for a grand ball, with innumerable jewels, the chief of which was a pendant that hung into her bosom and terminated in the most prodigious carbuncle I have ever seen, or ever heard tell of.

" ' "And now, sir," said she, "you have the right to

know who I am, and why I must demand that you be worthy of my trust; for the favor I have to ask of you may seem a slight thing, but I had rather lose my life than entrust my treasure to anyone unworthy. When you know the facts of the case, sir, you will understand what I mean.

" ' "My father, sir, was a gentleman who, if he was not worthy to be denominated *rich*, was at least comfortable in life, save that he had lost the one comfort for which he would have exchanged all the others; that is, his wife, my mother, who died when I was but an infant. He always showed the most tender regard for me, and (you will pardon a tear or two) he made sure that I lacked nothing which could tend to my happiness.

" ' "Nevertheless, as his only daughter, I was perforce much alone, and as I grew into a young woman, I was much addicted to long walks in the country round about our house. On one of those perambulations I met a young man walking the other way; we talked; we parted with the intention of meeting again on the morrow; and that night, sir, I thought of nothing but Christian (for Christian was the name of this young man), and in the morning counted the hours till I should meet him again. I shall be brief: we met each day after that, and the more I saw of him, the more my heart yearned for him. Nor did he appear to be without feeling for me; a thousand times he seemed on the verge of speaking his heart, and a thousand times stopped himself, until at last I could forbear no longer, and spoke to him boldly:

" ' " 'If you have somewhat to say to me, Christian,' said I, 'let not doubt stand in your way; for believe me, my disposition is such that I would hear whatever you would say most willingly.'

" ' "At this he sighed piteously and replied, 'Alas, dear Eleanor, would that I could speak what is in my heart; but if I were to do so, it would mean death to one who in no wise deserves to die.'

" ' " 'What can you mean by that?' I asked. 'Have you a wife already? For if you have, I conjure you to return to her at once and—'

" ' " 'I have no wife,' he said, interrupting me, 'but what I have is far more of an impediment: indeed, I should not scruple to call it a curse.'

" ' " 'No curse,' said I, 'is without hope, so long as we trust in God and despair not.'

" ' " 'My curse, however,' said he, 'is so nearly hopeless that despair is but reason; for it can be broken in only one way, and that a very unlikely one. Yet until the curse is broken, the very night I take a wife, an innocent man must die the most ignominious of deaths.'

" ' "I own that my heart sank at these words, but I persisted in believing that no curse could be without its remedy. 'How can this be?' I asked. 'Is there nothing within your power,—or—or mine,—which would lift this terrible curse from your head?'

" ' " 'Whether it be within your power I shall leave you to judge,' said he, 'when you have heard my tale, which is one of the most marvelous, and yet one of the most tragic, ever told by mortal lips.

" ' " 'I was the youngest son of a gentleman who, though he possessed many virtues, had a weakness for cards, so that he had squandered most of his fortune by the time I reached my majority. Having no other prospects, I determined to go to sea, and found a place aboard a ship owned by a prosperous wine-merchant. The duties were hard, but I was capable, and had fate not made other plans for me, I might still be a sailor today.

" ' " 'On my very first voyage, however, a tempest arose from the west, and buffeted our poor ship so severely that we were constrained to toss our cargo over the rail. When it came to the last cask, however, the merchant was so reluctant to part with it that he and the captain began a struggle that might had terminated with the death of one of them, have Nature herself not intervened by giving the boat such a toss at that moment that the barrel flew overboard on its own. At this the merchant was so wildly distraught that he began tearing his hair and shouting at the sailors to leap after the cask; and, finding no one willing to do so, he rushed against me, and, before I knew what he was about, had thrust me overboard. I struggled in the water and called for help, but in vain; the ship and I were so rapidly parted that no one could even contemplate my rescue. The cask, however, was floating close at hand, and I was able to haul myself up on it and ride out the tempest in that manner.

" ' " 'For two days I floated on that cask, which I dared not pierce for fear of sinking it. A merciful Providence, after the tempest, sent me occasional light rains, which, forming puddles on the top of the cask, gave me sufficient fresh water to drink. On the third day, I spotted an island, and to my inexpressible joy the wind and current carried me straight to the sandy shore, where I was deposited gently by the lapping waves.

" ' " 'Having thanked the Almighty for delivering me from the grasp of the sea, I took a look at my surroundings. The beach was bordered by a forest of palms and tropical trees, which I hoped might yield some sort of fruit; and indeed so it proved. So delighted was I by my discovery that I must have spent half an hour picking the grape-like berries of a species of palm before I noticed that, in the distance, I could hear the sound of rushing water—not the sea, but a steady sound from the interior of the island. Following the sound, I made my way through the verdant forest, until I came upon a scene that took my breath away; for there was a cascade of water at least a hundred feet high, and beside it a ruined temple festooned with barbarous but skillful carvings. Having drunk my fill of the clear water, I turned my attention to the exotic beauty of the temple, which was somewhat overgrown with vines, but still intact enough that the artistic taste of the architect and sculptors was evident. Monkeys chattered at me from the roof, and birds called from the trees, but there was no evidence that any man had set foot here within recent memory.

" ' " 'Enough of the roof was left that it seemed to me the temple would make an admirable shelter for the night. I entered, and found myself between two rows of columns, each column covered with intricate reliefs, and the whole interior drawing the eye to a statue of a woman or goddess at the other end. The woman was represented as seated, and even in that position the statue was at least fifteen feet high; it was of remarkable beauty; but what captivated me most was the way the eyes appeared to glow with a deep red light. As I approached more nearly, I perceived that the apparent glow was the glinting of two prodigious carbuncles which served the statue for eyes.

"'" 'I am not by nature a greedy man, but it seemed to me that two such jewels in a temple long abandoned were doing no one any good, and therefore might as well belong to me as to anyone else. I approached the statue, scattering a troop of monkeys, and began to climb it; and I was just stretching forth my hand to grasp the carbuncle in the left eye when a voice right beside me spoke:

"'" '" 'Tis not for mortal hands to touch the eye of the goddess!"

"'" 'I looked, but saw only a monkey sitting on the shoulder of the statue. "Who spoke?" I asked, and you may be sure that I was quite astonished when the monkey replied,

"'" '"I spoke—I, the guardian of the temple."

"'" '"But you are a monkey," said I, lowering myself to sit on the knee of the statue. "How is it that you speak, and in my own tongue?"

"'" '"That," replied the monkey, "is my curse, and my blessing, and I cannot explain more, unless I tell you my history."

"'" '"Nothing would delight me more," said I; "for until now I believed myself alone on this island."

"'" '"Then I shall be happy to tell you," said the monkey, sitting on the other knee of the statue. "I was not always a monkey. I was born a man like you, and in the course of time became the priest of this temple. I performed my duties, I believe, most assiduously; and the temple prospered under my care, until one day three men came to the island from far away, and stopped at my temple, evidently with the intention of persuading me to purchase something from them.

" ' " ' " 'I,' said the first, 'am a seller of hock, which is without a doubt the finest wine in the world.'

" ' " ' " 'Begging your pardon, sir,' said the second, 'but I contend that the claret of the blessed land of Bordeaux, which I have the honor to sell, surpasses all other wines whatsoever.'

" ' " ' " 'Neither of them,' said the third, 'can hold a candle to my Madeira.' " ' " '

"And that, gentlemen, is the story my brother Lawrence told me," Washington concluded.

There was silence in the room for half a minute, and then Parson Weems demanded, "What? Where is the rest of it? What of the priest who turned into a monkey?"

"And the curse of the man who must die an ignominious death?" added Susanna.

"And the beautiful red-haired lady?"

"With the prodigious carbuncle pendant?"

"And the ball gown on a stormy night?"

"And her love for the cursed young man?"

"And the innkeeper who must prove himself worthy?"

"And the cask of the best wine in the world?"

"Which he can know is the best without tasting it?"

"And the three men who wagered their night's lodging?"

"That was the way the story always ended when Lawrence told it," said Washington. "I remember specifically because that was always where his wife came in and said, 'Lawrence! Are you filling little Georgie's head with that nonsense again? You know what my Uncle Henry said about those stories. He said, "I met a man once who started to tell a story that went like this: 'Once there—' " ' "

"No!" cried Susanna. Then, seeing that all eyes had turned to her, she added, "I'm sorry. I don't know what came over me."

The arrival of the French changed the balance of the war considerably. The British evacuated Philadelphia almost immediately, and French fleets gave the British navy no end of trouble on the seas. Furthermore, the discipline introduced by Baron von Steuben had a salutary effect on our army. By coordinating their efforts to drop the Baron down wells, tar and feather him, &c., the men learned to work together as a unit.

For three more years the fortunes of war favored first one side and then the other, but it was becoming more and more difficult for the British to hold any temporary gains they had made. Eventually, when the news came that Cornwallis had landed his army in Virginia, it seemed that the time had come for a decisive stroke.

CHAPTER X.

New-York or Virginia?—Susanna presents the case for Virginia.—Plans for surrounding Cornwallis.—Susanna suggests amending the plans.—Surrender of Cornwallis.—Army discontented.—Plot to make Washington king.—Washington's retirement.

WE were now presented with a dilemma. Part of the British force was bottled up in New-York, where it might be possible, with the aid of the French fleet, to lay siege to them. The greater part, however, was in Virginia, where Cornwallis was perhaps planning a blow against Richmond, and thus might at a stroke cut off the South.

"To retake New-York," I pointed out, "would be a great boost to American spirits."

"But the army in Virginia," Susanna said, "may do us more damage than the loss of New-York ever did, or even the loss of Philadelphia, which after all was only temporary. I think—begging your pardon, Chr— Mr. Gist—that we ought to strike boldly against Cornwallis; we may at least prevent him from cutting off the Carolinas and Georgia, and if we are bold enough, and fortunate enough, we might defeat Cornwallis altogether. Such a victory would, in effect, win the war, as without Cornwallis' army the British could have no hope of success."

"It sounds very well," said Washington, "but how

are we to be sure of victory against so great an army? Cornwallis has greater numbers on his side."

"The French fleet, sir, will be essential," replied Susanna. "Cornwallis, we hear, has taken a position on the peninsula. If the French can prevent his escape by water, and prevent his being reinforced or resupplied, then we need only block the land routes, and we have him."

This seemed like good advice to Washington, and so Admiral de Grasse was summoned to a meeting with the General, at which La Fayette was also present, along with Susanna and me. We unrolled a large map of the peninsula between the York and James rivers, and the three great leaders studied it in intense silence for a while. At last Washington spoke.

"If we dispose our soldiers here, on the north and east, with Fayette's French army on the south, then you, Admiral, should be able to cut off Cornwallis completely by water to the west."

"Yes," de Grasse agreed, "the plan, it is excellent. He shall not escape us, by blue."

Susanna looked down at the map. "I believe, sirs, that you have mistaken the water for the land, and the land for the water. These wavy lines here, you see, indicate the water; the land is this area behind them, here."

"Ah!" said Washington. "Thank you, Phillips. Well spotted. That is important information, and complicates the strategy considerably. We cannot expect the men to stand very long in water that is possibly up to their necks, or even over their heads. We shall need to make some adaptations; perhaps some sort of bridge or pier assembly, or better yet a series of floating wooden platforms with which we can surround the peninsula on three sides, and on which the men can stand dryshod for an indefinite period of time. It will require a good bit of wood, which will require a good bit of labor; although the labor will be hastened considerably if we can find any large stands of wild cherry. That will do for the army; but, unless I am very much mistaken, the disposition of the fleet will require at least as much thought and labor, if not more."

"Very assuredly," the Admiral agreed. "I believe that a construction of the rollers, made perhaps of the trunks of the trees, will be necessary for the placing of the ships in position, if indeed suitable trees find themselves nearby."

"Well, there fortune favors us," said Washington. "Tidewater Virginia has many stands of pine that grow straight and tall, with few branches until very near the top; such trees would, it seems to me, make admirable rollers for our purposes."

Susanna was sitting with her head down, her eyes closed, and her fingers on her temples; but now she spoke again. "If I may be so bold, sirs, it might be better to reverse the positions of the army and the fleet."

The General and the Admiral both looked at her blankly for a moment; then Washington spoke slowly and cautiously. "Do you mean, the army on the land, and the navy in the water?"

"Yes, sir," Susanna said with care and patience. "Each force deployed in its native element, so to speak."

"My word, Phillips! How much simpler that makes

everything! You see, Admiral, why I insist on having Captain Phillips present whenever we discuss strategy. *Captain* Phillips? No, sir—Phillips, you are promoted to colonel as of this instant. We'll skip lieutenant colonel—no point in lingering there, eh, Phillips? Well done."

Later, as the meeting adjourned, I heard Admiral de Grasse ask Washington in a lowered voice, "That so brilliant young officer, the Colonel Phillips—is it that he perhaps appears pale to you?"

"I have often worried about that myself," Washington replied, "but it seems to be his natural complexion. If he were not so valuable to me, I should insist that he take a few weeks' rest; but, between us, Admiral, there are days when I do verily believe that our success in this war depends upon young Phillips."

"It can be that you there have reason, General," said the Admiral. "The army on the land and the navy in the water! Sacred blue! It is brilliant in its simplicity."

As soon as it was practical, therefore, the French fleet set off for the Chesapeake; meanwhile the combined American and French armies marched southward. Everything went according to plan. Admiral de Grasse was in position with his fleet; the combined armies blocked the land route on the peninsula. Cornwallis was surrounded, and unless he fought his way up the peninsula, or unless a large British fleet defeated the French, he was helpless.

"And now what shall we do?" Washington asked at the council of war he had called.

"Nothing," Susanna suggested.

"Nothing? But it seems to me that the 'nothing'

strategy was ineffective at New-York, and I thought we had given it up."

"There are times when nothing is effective, and times when it is not effective," Susanna explained with all the patience in her power. "When something has to be done, then nothing will not do. But there are times when circumstances favor patience, and at such times waiting is preferable to action, which may risk an undesirable result. I believe this is one of those times. Provoking a battle risks defeat; keeping Cornwallis bottled up in the peninsula must deplete his resources and eventually induce him to surrender."

"My word!" said Washington, "who would have thought that nothing would be so much more complicated than something?"

Hamilton spoke up. "It's all very well to do nothing when nothing can be done, Su— uh, Colonel Phillips. But at any moment a British fleet may arrive in the bay, and then everything depends on the French ships, which may not be able to hold off a sufficiently powerful attack. Cornwallis knows this, and therefore Cornwallis will never surrender. It seems to me, therefore, that an immediate attack—"

"Excuse me, General," said a young lieutenant who had appeared behind Washington.

"Just a moment, Hamilton," said Washington, and he turned to the lieutenant. "What have you to report?"

"Lord Cornwallis is here, sir. He says he would like to surrender, if it's not too much trouble."

"Tell him it's really no trouble at all," said Washington. "I'll be with him directly, as soon as I've heard what Hamilton has to say." The lieutenant went off to deliver Washington's reply, and Washington turned back to face Hamilton. "Now, Hamilton," Washington said, "please continue what you were saying, and forgive the interruption."

"As I say," Hamilton resumed, "I believe Cornwallis, in his present circumstances, will never surrender; and it behooves us, therefore—"

"But, Hamilton," Parson Weems interrupted him, "Cornwallis is surrendering right now."

"But that is a mere *fact*," Hamilton replied. "My argument is founded upon *reason*."

"Then, since the facts demand our attention now," said Susanna, "let us attend to them, and we may reserve reason for our leisure."

"Well said, Phillips," Washington concurred. "For there is a wise old saying—" He produced the copybook, and we waited for him to find the page, which had become more and more difficult for him to do as his fingers increased in size. "Here it is: 'Do not jog the desk on which another is writing.' I find it useful to have a fund of these proverbs ready to hand, so to speak, for they distill the wisdom of our elders to its essence. Let us now receive Lord Cornwallis as gentlemen."

The men had helpfully found Cornwallis a barrel to stand on, so that he and Washington could see eye to eye. He was waiting there, and Washington immediately engulfed Cornwallis' hand in his own.

"General," said Washington, "welcome to our camp."

"General Washington, sir," replied Cornwallis, "it is a great pleasure to make your acquaintance at last."

"Oh, I know what you mean. I've been looking forward to meeting you for ages. One never really gets to know a man when one is only firing cannonballs at him. I hope you don't take it too personally, by the way—the cannonballs, I mean, and the defeat and such."

"Certainly not. I have long since learned to expect that I shall often suffer such reverses, which I attribute entirely to the machinations of Willoughby."

"Willoughby?" asked Washington.

"My mortal enemy—the most fiendishly devious and diabolically wicked stoat ever born. Of course he is not—

"—not visible in the strict sense! Ah, Cornwallis, I know exactly what you mean!"

"Of course you do, sir! I know that a man of your talents must have the same experience. It is the very mark of a commander's greatness that he is pursued throughout his career—"

"—by the forces of envy and malice—"

"—personified in a malevolent invisible animal!" they both finished together.

"Mine is a mule named Irving," Washington said.

"General Washington, it is a positive honor to surrender to a soldier of your caliber. I hope we can settle on gentlemanly terms."

"Oh, yes, of course. I think it will be sufficient if you give me your word not to have anything more to do with fighting against the United States, and then you can be on your way."

"My word as a gentleman," said Cornwallis, extending his hand.

"I accept your word," said Washington, taking the

offered hand.

"But—" Hamilton sputtered, but Susanna and I both gestured to him to keep quiet.

"But how," he continued quietly to us, "I mean—what guarantee do we have that he'll keep his word?"

"He'll keep his word," Susanna insisted.

"But how do you know that?" Hamilton demanded in a hoarse whisper.

"I know it because he's just as much of an imbecile as Washington is," she replied. "And I sometimes wish the world were filled with such imbeciles."

As Susanna had expected, the victory over Cornwallis virtually ended the war. It was true that no treaty of peace had been signed, and Sir Henry Clinton in New-York refused to recognize the de-facto victory of the American side, continuing to occupy the city with such forces as he had; but the United States could get along very well without the city of New-York, and did so for the next two years. Nor did Clinton ever admit defeat: he is still there, in a small house on Wall-street, with two aged captains for company, and occasionally issues orders to occupy Hartford or Albany or whatnot, which his captains receive with deference and alacrity, without, however, setting foot out the front door.

The army now had nothing to do, and idle men began to consider more carefully the question of their payment. Once again the Congress attempted to pay them in paper money, which the men rejected as not worth so much as the same paper without any printing on it. So discontented were the men that they began to speak openly of marching to Annapolis (where the Congress was meeting at the time) to have Washington made king: for they imagined that, once granted royal power, Washington would not be long in finding the means to pay them in specie. This plot came to the ears of Washington himself, who mentioned it over the Madeira one evening after supper in the old brick church he had made his headquarters, it being the only nearby building where his ten-foot figure could be comfortably accommodated. We had made a special table for him, with a chair his own height and a set of benches with stepladders so that we could all sit at the same table with him.

"Of course we do have the Articles of Confederation," Washington said, "but I believe those must be regarded as a temporary measure. If we are to have a single nation rather than a rabble of thirteen unrelated States, we must adopt a form of government conducive to unity. A monarchy would, obviously, serve that purpose, and a careful choice of monarch is vital to the viability of our union. It ought to be—"

"Yes, we have been over this ground before," said Susanna, "and we know that it ends at the conclusion that our ideal monarch would look very much like you, General Washington. But of course one doesn't put oneself forward as seeking the kingship."

"One doesn't?"

"Modesty and diffidence are considered greatly desirable qualities in monarchs. Indeed, a monarch's impassivity is precisely what makes him look like a monarch. It is essential to show that you do not desire the position of king, and that you would accept it only with extreme reluctance."

"Do you think so? Yes, I can see how that might be true."

"If you would like, I could draft you a few remarks, which you might use when the occasion presents itself."

"Oh, would you, Phillips? That would be very kind of you."

Later, as Susanna sat at the desk in our chamber writing some remarks for Washington to deliver extemporaneously, I asked her, "What exactly are you up to?"

"Kiss my neck and don't ask questions," she replied.

It was not long before the expected occasion did present itself. A gathering of junior officers and enlisted men formed in front of Washington's church headquarters, and when Washington appeared at the door, they presented him with a set of resolutions calling upon him to lead the army to Annapolis and declare himself king.

Fortunately, Washington had laboriously memorized Susanna's response. "Gentlemen," said he, "I am sensible of the honor you do me in making this request, but at the same time I find it impossible to acquiesce. Are you not aware that we have spent seven years fighting a war not only against George III, but against the very institution of monarchy? Why, every man I see before me is a king on a throne of gold; for in our republic, gentlemen, the power rests with the people themselves, and not with some class of arbitrarily distinguished men who have no more natural parts than you have, and perhaps a great deal less good sense. Would you have me elevate myself above you, when we have fought so long and so hard for the principle that all men are created equal? No, gentlemen, so reluctant am I to abandon our shared republican principles that I could never desire the position of king, and only the direst circumstances would induce me to accept such an honor."

At the conclusion of this speech, the men gave a mighty cheer, which pleased Washington very much; but what did not please him nearly so much was that they took him at his word, and did not make him king.

"Well," said Susanna, "we tried our best."

"We did," Washington agreed; "the principle was inarguably sound, and our lack of success can only be attributed to the malice of Irving, who would not wish to see me crowned king if he could prevent it. Irving will yet be the death of me, you may be certain of that. But though he may prevent my elevation to the throne, I hope he will not be able to prevent my enjoying the fruits of our hard-won victory. The time has come for me to retire from public life, and to give my full attention to the development of my estate at Mount Vernon."

With this surprising announcement, Washington abandoned all hope of becoming King of the United States. Shortly afterward, a formal peace was concluded, and Washington traveled to Annapolis to resign his commission before the Congress. He was able to witness personally the evacuation of New-York by the British, with the exception of Clinton and the two captains aforesaid; and then he retired to Mount Vernon, fully intending to remain there for the rest of his life.

CHAPTER XI.

*Washington's private life.—Failings of the Articles of
Confederation.—Constitutional Convention called.—
Seating difficulties.—One dollar, one vote rejected.—
Question of apportioning representation.—The Three-
Fifths Compromise.—Constitution adopted.*

OVER the next few years Susanna and I saw Washington frequently, but we were not in constant attendance as before. We took up residence in my house on
Prince-street in Alexandria, and about a year afterward Susanna gave birth to our son Crispus Attucks
Gist, named for her martyred friend in Boston. A year
later, our daughter Jane Adams Gist arrived, whom
we named for Mrs. Adams because she and Susanna
had conceived a warm friendship. After that, although
we certainly did everything in our power to encourage
them, no more children arrived, and we assumed—
mistakenly, as we were to discover much later—that,
for whatever reason, Susanna was incapable of bearing any more.

Parson Weems had retired to Georgetown across
the river to work on his tracts, of which he issued a
steady stream: "On the Falsity of All Human Tradi-
tions, Saving Certain Exceptions Herein Enumer-
ated"; "On the Poor Fashion Sense of the Romish Hi-
erarchy"; "An Inquiry into the Scandalously Immoral
Behavior of Certain Orders of Nuns, with Numerous

Woodcuts"; "Whether the Pope Possesses a Hidden Tail, with a Commentary on the Seventeenth Chapter of Revelation"; and other similar titles, most of which sold very well, assuring their author a comfortable living. He had them printed at the Gazette office in Alexandria, and would generally stop for dinner with us after a day at the printer's; I was always glad to see him, and Susanna was at least polite to him, though she was not as fond of him as I was.

Of course we were frequent guests at Mount Vernon. Washington was not a man to forget loyal friends, and I believe Susanna, Parson Weems, and I saw more of him than did all the great men of the age who stopped to pay tribute to the greatest of them all, and to seek his advice, an experience that usually left them more baffled than they had been before they arrived.

In short, I will say that my own life was very pleasant in the few years after our victory in the War of Independence; and so, I believe, was Washington's. Our country, however, was suffering.

The difficulty, as all agreed, lay in the Articles of Confederation. That agreement, hastily put together when the states were in the throes of their war for independence, gave us a national government that existed only at the whim of the states; and we soon discovered that the states could be quite whimsical. The Congress depended on the contributions of the states for its budget, and there were no consequences for states that failed to make the agreed-on contributions. Moreover, the Empire of Rhode Island and Providence Plantations showed a distressing tendency to bully the other states, which the Articles of Confederation provided no means of counteracting. Clearly some revisions were necessary, and it must be soon, preferably before Connecticut declared war on Rhode Island.

Thus the Congress voted to call a convention in Philadelphia for the purpose of revising the Articles of Confederation, and naturally Virginia chose Washington as one of her delegates.

"I should like to have you and Phillips with me," Washington said when he told me about the convention. "Your steadying influence, and his incisive mind, will be of great use to me in Philadelphia. We ought to have Parson Weems as well, if he can spare the time, for a bit of spiritual advice would not come amiss at this important juncture."

"I'll have to ask Su— Phillips, but for my part I should be glad to offer whatever assistance I can give."

Susanna was reluctant to leave the children for so long, though we had a capable and intelligent nurse whom they loved, and who would be more than adequate to the task of caring for them. "But on the other hand, if Virginia has chosen Washington, the other states have probably chosen the usual lot of imbeciles; and if I can be there to speak for sanity— Very well; we'll go, and the children will come with us."

"Is that wise?" I asked.

"Crispus is already speaking in complete sentences," said Susanna. "Perhaps he can draft some of the articles."

So it was done. We made slow progress to Philadelphia with Jane and Crispus, but they enjoyed the new sights along the way, and certainly Susanna and I were happier for not worrying about what might be happening to them at home.

When we arrived in Philadelphia, we found the preparations for the convention already in progress, and already encountering their first difficulty. Washington had grown considerably since the successful conclusion of the war. He was now a little over thirteen feet tall, and while this height presented no architectural problem in the ample chamber chosen for the convention, it was clear that none of the furniture was at all adequate to Washington's current dimensions.

Here was a problem the convention would have to solve before it could even begin to address the perceived weaknesses in the Articles of Confederation. It was imperative that at least one chair be made in Washington's size. Yet no one wished to be the one who drew attention to Washington's unusual height. We all preferred not to mention it, and I was never quite sure how much Washington himself was aware of his own size. Furthermore, the pride of some of the other delegates would hardly admit of one delegate's having an obviously larger seat than the rest. The representatives from Rhode Island, where size has often been a sensitive question, threatened to withdraw from the union altogether and form an independent and potentially hostile Empire if any Virginian sat in a chair whose dimensions exceeded those of the chairs occupied by Rhode Island by so much as a single inch.

In the end it was decided by the Standing Committee on Seating that all furniture in the hall should be so made as to accommodate any delegate up to fourteen feet tall. Thus the problem was addressed without any specific reference to Washington himself, and the feelings of smaller delegates were spared. Most of the delegates required stepladders, or for some of the more infirm hoisting tackle, to make the ascent into their seats; but the important thing was that harmony was preserved, and the convention was not irreparably split over questions of protocol before any of the more important issues had been dealt with.

Susanna and I did not attend the sessions with Washington, so we heard about the actual debates second-hand; but we heard them in great detail, for Washington loved to talk about them. The first debate, of course, was over the presidency of the convention, and as far as Washington was concerned there could be only one reasonable choice. Fortunately, he was able to make the other delegates see reason, or see how difficult it would be if they did not see things his way. The first day he came back to the inn where we were staying (a house with comfortably high fifteen-foot ceilings, and a large back parlor where we accommodated Washington by laying four beds side by side) to announce that he had been chosen president of the convention. Furthermore, he was quite pleased to find that his old friend Alexander Hamilton had come to the convention as the delegate from New-York state. "The men of New-York sent only one delegate," said Washington, "and in this I believe they have shown wisdom; for one Hamilton is worth half a dozen of the rest. I believe his 'one-dollar-one-vote' proposal has a very good chance of acceptance."

"One-dollar-one-vote?" I repeated.

"Hamilton explained it to me. It seems very clever.

Each man would have a voting power proportional to his wealth, so that the burden of government falls most heavily upon those who most naturally have an interest in the stability of the Union."

"I'd like to talk to Hamilton about that personally," said Susanna. I did not like the way the fingers of her right hand were closing into a fist.

"The thing that worries me," Washington continued, "is that the delegates from the Empire of Rhode Island and Providence Plantations have gone home and refused to have anything further to do with the convention. I hope that troublesome state is not bent on causing us more difficulties. We need the cooperation of all the states, for a civil war between Rhode Island and the other states would be destructive and unpleasant. However, we can only trust in our own wisdom to erect a government that will, by its obvious utility, recommend itself even to the mobs in Newport and Providence."

"Perhaps," Susanna suggested, "we ought to trust in God instead."

We did in fact see quite a bit of Mr. Hamilton as the days went on. He often dined with us, and he spoke of his plans for a government "of the wealthy, by the wealthy, and for the wealthy" with great enthusiasm. I kept one eye on Susanna's right fist, for there was something about Mr. Hamilton that unsettled her.

Eventually, however, it became clear that Hamilton's most audacious proposals would not gain the support of most of the states. Many of the delegates, indeed, were insisting that every man should have a vote.

"Why every man?" Susanna asked when Washington brought us this news.

"That is indeed the question Hamilton has been asking. He believes that at least a property requirement—"

"No, I mean, why should the franchise be limited to men?"

"What do you mean? Would you have horses and mules vote as well?"

"Why should women not vote for their elected representatives? In all matters with which this government is concerned, they are equally affected. It is their homes that will be taxed, their husbands and sons who will be sent to war; it is they who will suffer most from bad government and benefit most from good."

"Yes, Phillips," replied Washington, "but women have not the analytical capacity which you and I enjoy. Surely you, of all people, with your exceptionally keen mind, can appreciate that difference. Your suggestion of extending the franchise to horses and mules may, however, be worthy of consideration."

Susanna was about to say something in reply, but clearly thought better of it, and merely sat with her head down and her fingers on her temples. Many of her conversations with Washington seemed to end the same way.

The apportionment of representation in Congress was another difficulty that much concerned Washington. Susanna suggested an elegant compromise in which there would be two houses of Congress, like the House of Commons and the House of Lords, the one apportioned by population, and the other with equal representation from each state. This was eagerly adopted when Washington brought it up the next day, but then the question of how to determine the population of a state came up. The states of the South wished to have their slaves included; the states of the North, naturally, did not wish to concede so much influence to the South.

"They are still debating it—the representation question," Washington told us one evening.

"They seem to be unable to face the real question of slavery," said Susanna.

"And they have spent days debating," Washington continued, "with no result that I can see other than frayed tempers and a considerable diminution of the Madeira stock."

"It is because no one is bold enough to ask the real question," said Susanna. "Instead they will talk themselves in circles, never touching on the one thing no one dares mention, until they are so weary of talking that they will make some absurd compromise and decide that a slave counts as, oh, three-fifths of a person, and then call it a job well done and hope no one ever reads the text."

"Three-fifths of a person," Washington repeated quietly. And then he suddenly brightened. "My word, Phillips, what a mind you have! Yes, that's the answer!"

Susanna began to protest: "But I was just—"

"Yes, yes, it solves the problem perfectly—an almost mathematical balance between the regions!"

"But it's abs—"

"I must tell Hamilton at once!" He had risen and was already headed for the door, with that odd hunching walk he had developed in unconscious adaptation to the usual dimensions of interior doorways. "I don't know what we'd do without you, Phillips! This is the best idea you've had since that Electoral College thing." He ducked out the door.

"What? Wait—they adopted that too? But that was—"

The door closed.

"But that was a joke!" she almost wailed to the closed door. Then she turned to me. "Christopher, can we stop him?"

"I don't think anything can stop the General once he has an idea stuck in his head."

"But they're making a hash of my country, and it's all my fault!"

I stood and took her hand. "My dearest, the greatest minds of these United States are gathered here in Philadelphia. Every point in this new form of government is accepted only after mature deliberation."

"Yes, but..." She laid her head on my shoulder. "But the greatest minds in these United States are all a bunch of imbeciles."

Susanna was not well pleased when, the next day, Washington came back from the day's session with the news that the "three-fifths" compromise had been accepted with minimal debate. She had to endure Washington's congratulations over dinner, which she did with silent mortification; and Washington kept bringing up the subject for the rest of the evening, so that Susanna found it necessary to retire early on the excuse of a headache.

She was still awake when I joined her in bed, and she was still feeling gloomy. "I've made a mess of the

Constitution," she said as we lay in the dark (speaking quietly, so as not to wake the children), "and there's nothing I can do to change it."

"The Constitution need not be perfect," I assured her. "It will still be better than the fraying fabric of Confederation."

"But I've just increased the power of the slaveholders by an enormous amount. Slavery will simply wither away, you keep saying. Do you see it withering now?"

"With a strong federal government, the men of the North and East who oppose slavery will find partners in the South, and the institution will be ended peacefully, with minimal disruption. The alternative is disunion and bloodshed. You may have been responsible for saving the Union, Susanna, and averting a bloody civil war. In a few decades at most, slavery will be extinct, and—"

"And all the men and women and little helpless children who died as slaves will look down from heaven and say, 'Thank you, Susanna Gist—thank you for letting us die without tasting freedom. Thank you for making sure—"

She stopped. There was a loud whooping coming from downstairs, accompanied by rhythmic pounding. Washington was laughing.

"Someone must have told him a joke this afternoon," I remarked.

The whooping continued, and then we very distinctly heard him shouting, "Three-fifths of a person!" Then more pounding, as of heels kicking on the floor.

Susanna turned over and pulled the coverlet over her head.

There were times, indeed, when it seemed to all of us that the convention must end in failure, and that no agreement could ever be reached among the states. Nature, however, proved our ally. The insupportable heat of a Philadelphia summer was now fully upon us. Curiously, the children seemed to grow more cheerful as the heat grew more oppressive; but Washington reported that the delegates were withering. More and more provisions were accepted in this new constitution simply because it was easier to say "yes" than to debate in the sweltering furnace where the convention was meeting. Washington told us that the delegates from Massachusetts had nearly got a constitutional prohibition of red chowder written into the document before Mr. Hamilton woke from his afternoon somnolence and vetoed it.

When at last the Constitution of the United States had been accepted by the convention, we returned home and awaited the verdict of the states. It took a year and a half, but at last the Constitution was ratified by the state conventions. Now there was much to be done. A whole national government had to be built from the very foundation. But in Washington's mind there was really only one interesting question: who was to take on the exalted and onerous duties reserved in the Constitution for the President of the United States?

CHAPTER XII.

*Washington for President.—Mr. Hamilton's plan for
electing him.—New terminology for a new form of government.—Posters, broadsides, and articles in the papers.—Campaign tour.—Debate with Adams.—Washington elected.*

To THE question of who should be our president there
could, in Washington's mind, be only one answer.
How to arrange the desired result, however, was not
completely obvious. The Constitution had created a
mechanism by which a president would be chosen:
viz., Susanna's "Electoral College," a term I quickly
learned not to mention in her presence. But what was
an Electoral College, and how did one come to be?
The Constitution's rules were simple and direct, but
only because they left many questions unanswered.
When the people chose electors, were they to choose
men whose judgment they trusted on account of long
experience and preeminence in wisdom? Phrased in
those terms, the question answered itself quickly. It
was decided by no one, or by everyone at once, that
the people would choose men who had already made
up their minds as to which candidate they would
choose, and would not change their minds under any
circumstances, no matter what new evidence might
come to light.

There were many men who thought they might be

exactly the man required for this new position of President. Fortunately Washington had a weapon in his arsenal that could not be matched by any of his opponents. Mr. Hamilton had already concluded that his own prospects of advancement depended upon Washington's being elected President, and he threw himself into the project with his customary enthusiasm.

"We need to make sure you're appealing to all demographics," Hamilton explained over Madeira on the back porch at Mount Vernon.

"What are demographics?" Washington naturally asked.

"That's a term I've come up with on my own. It literally means 'people-writing.' "

"You want me to write on people?"

"No, you misunderstand—"

"I usually just sign their autograph albums, and that makes them happy enough."

"It's not about writing on—"

"I'd think the quill would tickle them terribly."

"Please try to—"

"There was one young woman in Annapolis who made a request I considered somewhat immodest, but even that was on fabric."

"Look, there are—"

"And the ink feathered, so that to my mind the signature was spoiled, but on the other hand I should hope that not many people will see that much of her anyway."

"It doesn't mean writing on people," Hamilton said. "It means writing *about* people."

"Oh, I see," said Washington. "Well, really, when I think about it, I do seem to write mostly about people, except for Irving of course. That is, when I do write. Well, I shall be very glad to have a new word for it."

"Let me begin again," said Hamilton. "There are many different kinds of people, and we want to make sure you appeal to all of them. The best way to do that is with targeted advertising, as I call it."

"Do you—"

"And I'm not shooting anything!" Hamilton explained quickly. "Let me show you what I mean. What sort of people do you think go to cheap inns and taverns?"

"Well," said Washington, "I should think they would be people with little money who like to drink."

"There you are, then," said Hamilton. 'We put up a poster in every cheap tavern: "Share a Drink with Washington—A Man of the People, for the People, Protecting Your Interests from the Rich.' And then what sort of people go to the races?"

"Mostly wealthy planters," Washington replied.

"So we put up posters wherever the races meet: 'Washington—The Prince of Planters, Protecting Your Interests from the Mob.' You see how it works. You aim, so to speak, your advertisements at the people who are likely to see them in the place where we hang them. Thus your advertisements are *targeted*, as I call it."

"But it seems to me that you have General Washington acting in two entirely contradictory ways," said Susanna. "You have him protecting the poor against the rich, and the rich against the poor."

"I prefer to say 'complementary' rather than 'contrary,' " said Hamilton. "Like St. Paul, you become all things to all men."

"Oh, well, if it's in *Scripture*," said Washington.

"We're simply broadening your appeal by the Pauline method, as it were. Similarly, in the New England states, we shall have posters to tell the people that Washington is the protector of shipping and manufacturing interests against the rich plantation-owners, and in the South, of course, we shall be careful to say that Washington, the man of the South, will protect Southern interests against Northern plutocrats."

"Plutocrats?" Weems asked.

"It's another word I've come up with on my own," Hamilton said proudly. "It means rich people with too much influence."

"My word, Hamilton, you certainly are enriching our American language," said Washington. "Why, if we keep adding words at this rate, no one will be able to understand us at all."

"We explain what they mean as we introduce them," Hamilton responded. "I have a list, you see, and I add to it every day." He shuffled downward in his stack of papers until he found the one he was looking for. "Here it is."

Washington took the paper, which looked tiny in his hand, and examined it closely. "Well, you certainly have been busy, Hamilton. You have some fine words here, if I'm any judge of words. Like '*ee*-lights,' for example. What are '*ee*-lights'?"

"That's 'ay-*leets*,' " said Hamilton. "It's a word I borrowed from the French."

"Oh, well, I suppose if we pillage foreign languages, there's no end to the number of words we can come up with. I thought you were just making them up out of your own head, like 'sizzwappler.' "

" 'Sizzwappler'? What's that?"

"It's a word I just made up out of my own head," Washington explained.

"But, you see, these words are formed on regular principles out of the materials already afforded us by the Saxon, French, Latin, or Greek."

"It seems like a great deal of work to have to know four languages just to make up words in English. I think my method is much simpler. What does 'ay-*leets*' mean, anyway?"

"It means people who are better educated, with more wisdom and understanding, than the average man."

"Oh, I see. So you want to tell the people that I am one of these ay-*leets*."

"No! People hate the elites. They don't want anyone to be wiser or to know more than they do. They want a leader who's as stupid and ignorant as they are."

"But then why would they want someone like me?" asked Washington.

A brief silence followed, and then Hamilton explained, "It's simply a matter of image." He pointed to the word "image" in his list. "We want to create an image of you as a man of the people."

"You mean like a statue?"

"No!" Hamilton put some effort into getting his annoyance under control; it could perhaps be unwise to be too short with a man who was three times his height. "You have doubtless imagined, say, George the Third in your mind."

"Oh, yes," said Washington. "I picture him with

long ears that stand up and out from his head, a long muzzle, four hooves, a long and brushy tail..."

"You mean like a mule?"

"Precisely. I believe he shares many characteristics with my archnemesis Irving."

Hamilton looked blank for a moment, and then assimilated this new addition to the conversation and went on. "Well, that *image* in your mind stands in for King George. When you think of King George, that is what you think of. What we want to do is control the *image* the voters have of you in their minds. We want them to see the right image when they hear your name."

"Oh!" cried Washington, "so they can see me when I'm not there! That's extraordinary, Hamilton. It's a remarkable idea. A real sizzwappler. Do you have a word for that, too—people seeing me when I'm far away?"

"It's not really— Well, actually, I suppose it *is* seeing you when you're far away, isn't it? We could call it "teleoptics,' or 'proculovision.' "

"How about 'television'?" asked Washington. "I like the sound of that."

"No, you can't combine Greek and Latin parts that way. But you see the principle, don't you? When the ordinary tavern-goer thinks of you, we want him to think of someone like him—someone who hates the rich industrialists and planters and merchants and suchlike people and looks out for the interests of the ordinary man. When the planters think of you, we want them to see a rich planter who thinks the way they do and hates the common mob. That's what I mean by 'image.' "

"But the way you paint these images of me, I'm not sure I'd like me very much if I met me."

"We don't care what *you* think of you. We care what *they* think of you. We need to reach the people who will vote for the electors who will vote for Washington."

"And you will do this by putting up images of me?"

Hamilton looked blank again for a moment, and then said, "If necessary."

The only other candidate we really had to fear was John Adams, who was not nearly so well known as the General. But Hamilton was bent on leaving nothing to chance. Soon we began to see Washington-for-President broadsides and posters wherever we went. When Susanna and I took little Crispus and Jane for a walk down toward the docks, there were Washington's posters:

WASHINGTON

for

LOWER

TARIFFS

and

MARITIME

IMPROVEMENTS

Later Susanna asked Hamilton what he meant by "maritime improvements," and he replied, "It means whatever the shipping interests want it to mean."

Not long afterward, a poster appeared across from St. Paul's, very near our house:

DON'T LET THEM TAKE YOUR SLAVES
Vote for
WASHINGTON
Because when slavery is outlawed,
only outlaws will have slaves.

Susanna was especially enraged by this one because she already knew that Hamilton had sent to Boston to have posters put up with a very different message:

KEEP MASSACHUSETTS FREE
Vote for
WASHINGTON
Don't let slaveholders
control the confederation.

"How is that even logical?" she had demanded of Hamilton when he told us of the Boston posters. "Washington is a slaveholder himself, and you are asking them to put him at the head of the Union."

"The people will vote for the image," Hamilton had replied. "The man is immaterial."

Meanwhile Mr. Adams' campaign was not idle. A few days after Washington's first posters were put up, a small poster appeared on the wall of the Lyceum:

You Might Consider Voting
for
JOHN ADAMS
If It Is Not
Too Much Trouble.

We saw no other Adams posters, but the mere existence of this one raised Mr. Hamilton's ire to a frightening degree. "We must crush this Adams," he said when we were again gathered on the porch at Mount Vernon. "We must pound him into the earth until there is no life left in him."

"Mr. Hamilton," Washington said with obvious shock, "John Adams is a friend of mine, and no consideration could induce me to do him the least injury."

"I meant it metaphorically, of course," Hamilton said hastily. "Privately you and Mr. Adams may remain the best of friends. It is only in the political sense that we must beat him down and crush his bones to powder under our boots. That is what 'politics' *means*."

"I'm not sure I understand," said Washington. "What would we do to beat him down politically but not personally?"

"Well, for a start, we might place anonymous articles in the Gazette, which would soon be picked up by the papers from Boston to Savannah."

"I see. And what would these articles say?"

"Anything unflattering about Adams that would damage his reputation. We could question his masculinity, for example."

"Don't be absurd, Hamilton. Adams is as much a man as any of us here. I know a man when I see one; I can tell the difference."

Hamilton glanced helplessly at Susanna, but she gave him a look that would wither an oak tree.

"The content of the accusation is not important," Hamilton bravely continued. "In fact it will be more effective if we do not phrase the thing as an accusation. but rather as a question. "Is John Adams a Horse Thief?" You see we say nothing dishonest; we merely ask a question. Or, better yet, a denial: "Adams Denies Arson Charges, Say Campaign Insiders." We tell no untruth: in fact we specifically deny that Adams is an arsonist. Nothing could be more honest than that."

"But what do you accomplish by telling the voters that Mr. Adams has done nothing wrong?" I asked.

"Ah, but we do not precisely tell them that he has done nothing wrong. We tell them that he has *denied* doing something wrong, and they will conclude from that that someone has accused him of doing it, and then they will wonder, Did he do it? And there will be a good number of them who think, in the words of the old adage, 'Where there's smoke—' "

" '—permission ought to be asked of the ladies.' Yes, I am familiar with the proverb," Washington said. "But something about this makes me uneasy, Hamilton. Is it not possible to win the office of President simply by giving the public a candid assessment of my intelligence and abilities, and thus allowing the people to make an informed decision?"

Hamilton thought for a moment.

"No," he replied at last.

Soon Hamilton's anonymous articles began appearing in the Alexandria Gazette. As Hamilton had foretold, the articles were not long in being reprinted in Philadelphia, Charleston, Baltimore, New-York, Savannah, Hartford, and even as far west as Pittsburgh; or so I was told much later by a certain Mr. Brackenridge, who will appear later in these pages.

Not long after that, we began to hear the rumors in the usual gossip at the taverns and coffee-houses of

Alexandria, and even in church: *they say* that Adams stole twenty horses from a defenseless old widow in Quincy; *they say* that Adams has one-quarter African blood in his veins; *they say* that Adams wears a long coat to hide his pointed tail; *they say* all those things that Hamilton's articles specifically denied about Adams, which, as Hamilton had intended, introduced thoughts that had not previously been in the minds of the people. Adams and his friends wrote letters denying the rumors, but all their denials were merely favorable breezes under the wings of Rumor, and had the effect of spreading the stories farther and farther. In effect, Adams was doing Washington's campaigning for him.

Meanwhile, Hamilton arranged for Washington to travel up and down the country to meet the people face to face—"shaking hands and kissing babies," as Hamilton explained, although the latter part of the program was quickly abandoned when we discovered that the effect on babies of a fifteen-foot man bending down to kiss them was not uniformly positive. We traveled in a train of coaches and wagons, which Hamilton called a "cavalcade," that included a large number of correspondents for the various papers up and down the country. After Washington began to complain of back pain, we added a large crew of diggers, who would go ahead of us and prepare a nine-foot-deep trench for Washington to walk up and down in, so that he could greet the people who came to see him without bending over. Everywhere we stayed, of course, Washington put up one of his brass plaques, which were greatly prized by the communities; most of them appeared now on churches and meeting halls,

and not a few barns; which, but for the very most opulent planters' houses in the South, were generally the
only available buildings sufficiently large to accommodate Washington's current dimensions. We had to
send men ahead—"advance scouts," Hamilton called
them—to find such accommodations, and, after two
regrettable incidents that were much talked about
where they occurred, to make sure that the location
chosen for Washington's appearance before the crowd
was not dangerously near a cherry orchard.

As more and more writers for the weeklies joined
our cavalcade, their demands upon Washington's time
grew more and more inconvenient, until at last
Hamilton set aside certain times when all of them
could gather at once and ask the General whatever
questions occurred to them. Because of the press of
correspondents trying to push their way to the front,
these occasions quickly became known among the literary gentlemen as "press conferences." The usual
procedure was that one correspondent at a time
would be chosen to ask a question, to which Washington would give a reply, and then Hamilton, standing
on a raised platform beside him, would explain what
Washington meant by what he had said. It was not
obvious to Washington that these explanations were
truly representative of his own thoughts; but Hamilton gave him another lecture on the subject of "image," and Washington agreed because agreeing made
the lecture stop.

Hamilton's master stroke was to arrange a face-to-
face debate between Washington and Adams in Philadelphia. In this debate, certain correspondents from
the Philadelphia papers were permitted to ask ques-

tions, which both candidates answered extemporaneously. Mr. Adams answered every question intelli-
gently, and had all the information about tariffs,
diplomacy, commerce, finance, Indian affairs, and
turnpikes ready to hand. Washington had none of
that, with the result that his brief answers and irrele-
vant aphorisms held the attention of the audience,
and he was universally judged to be the winner of the
debate.

At last the great day came; the people went to the
polls in great numbers; they chose electors for Washington; and the General was ready to take his place as
the first President of the United States.

But if the electoral process was obscure, it was clar-
ity itself in comparison with the presidency. The Constitution specified a few duties of the President,
which, taken together, might occupy a day of his time
out of the month. What was the President supposed to
be doing the rest of the time?

CHAPTER XIII.

Washington considers presidential protocol.—Secret "tape" system in his office.—Hamilton invents a new currency.—Choosing a site for the capital.—Mr. Banneker and Mr. L'Enfant.—Washington's improvements to the plans.

THE first decision Washington made was that the President would have to reside wherever the Congress was. He took a house in New-York and removed the second floor to give him a more comfortable ceiling height (for he was now just under sixteen feet tall). The Constitution had made provision for a new capital, but where it would be had not yet been decided. Each state had its reasons why it ought to possess the new capital, and there were many debates to be had before a site could be chosen. Meanwhile, the Congress was still peripatetic; but it had settled in New-York for a while, which suited Washington, as he was hoping to take in a few more puppet-shows.

At Washington's earnest request, Susanna and I came to New-York as well, along with the children. He also induced Parson Weems to join us; and the evening Weems arrived, we spent two or three hours after supper discussing the protocol for the new office of the presidency.

"I thought perhaps," said Washington, "we ought to come up with a kind of manual of forms of address.

When the President is spoken of, for example, in what way is he styled? I had thought it might be something like "His Gracious and Exalted Majesty the President of the United States, by the Grace of God Defender of the Rights of the American People, Commander in Chief of the Army and Navy and of the Militias of the Several States, Appointer to Offices, Filler of Vacancies, Informer of the Congress as Regards the State of the Union, Arbiter of Opinions, Granter of Pardons, Maker of—"

"Do you think that might be somewhat cumbersome?" Susanna asked.

"Well, of course, the full title would be used only the first time the President was mentioned; after that, the title 'His Gracious and Exalted Majesty' would suffice."

"I was thinking perhaps 'Mr. President' would do," said Susanna.

"Is that not somewhat...common?" asked Washington.

"Not at all. Quite the reverse. In all the states of Europe, you will find gracious and exalted majesties, defenders of the faith, high and mighty autocrats, and so on. A man may rule a strip of land the size of a pocket-handkerchief, but his majesty is still gracious and exalted. Gracious and exalted majesties are a shilling a cartload. What no other country has is a President, a ruler whose power depends not on the number of titles he piles on top of his name, but on the genuine love of his people, whereof his very position is the proof and sign. When one has said 'President,' one has spoken a name whose luster eclipses all lesser titles, to which any addition must be a diminution."

"Do you really think so?" Washington asked, obviously impressed.

"So firmly do I believe it, that in the future, I will venture to say, other countries will have Presidents rather than kings, and the most powerful rulers in the world will affect the title we Americans have given to our executive."

"My word, Phillips!" cried Washington. "I had not thought of the thing in those terms, but 'Mr. President' it shall be!"

Some time later, after Washington had retired and we were walking back home to our lodgings, Parson Weems said, "That was very clever, Susanna—puncturing his bubble by pretending to inflate it."

"I had to do something," she replied, "and he's grown too big to be conveniently punched in the face."

A few days later, Washington was showing me the presidential office he had set up in his New-York residence, which would also serve as a kind of audience chamber. The best cabinetmakers in the city had been commissioned to make an immense desk and chair in Washington's own size. "Here," said Washington, "in the back of the house, I may meet privately with such men as I have business with, and we shall not be overheard or disturbed."

"But is it wise for the President to conduct business with no witnesses?" I asked. "I will not say that there are dishonest men in our government, but misunderstandings may arise, which, without a witness on record, may be difficult to settle."

"Ah," Washington said with a sly nod, "in fact I

have considered that eventuality;—or Hamilton has, which comes to the same thing." He pointed to his desk. "In this office I have installed a system that silently records every conversation."

"Every conversation?" I repeated incredulously. "But how is that possible?"

"You will, of course, keep this a secret as long as I am President," said Washington; and he led me over to his desk. Lifting the top of it entirely away, he pointed down. I stood on my toes and peered into the desk. There, inside the Washington-sized desk, was a man sitting at an ordinary desk with a quill, a big pot of ink, and a narrow roll of paper, which proceeded from under the right side of the desk, passed across the writing surface, and was wound on a big spool under the left side of the desk.

"Mr. Shelton here," Washington explained (and the man immediately started scribbling), "is a remarkably quick man with a quill. With a continuous roll of narrow paper, or 'tape,' as Hamilton calls it, he has no need to lose time changing sheets, and his shorthand can keep up with the fastest talker. Every conversation that takes place in this office is recorded on one of these 'tapes,' and I can retrieve the exact words that were spoken any time I like."

He set the top back down, and Mr. Shelton was completely hidden.

"But isn't it dark under there?" I asked. "How does he see?"

"I have no idea," Washington replied. He lifted the top of the desk again. "It seems light enough under there now." He set the top back down. "And the important thing is that all my presidential conversations are recorded on 'tape,' so that the chance of my being embarrassed in any way is virtually eliminated."

"And you don't worry that someone might use the very existence of such a record to embarrass you?"

"Gist, I hope I can say with confidence that I never say anything in this room of which I have cause to be ashamed. Indeed I find it difficult to imagine that the states would ever elect a man to the presidency who would be embarrassed by anything that might be recorded by such a system. The electoral mechanism is designed to select honorable men, and I have faith that it will continue to do so."

Meanwhile the business of creating a government occupied most of the meetings of Congress; and as Congress created the positions, the President was required to nominate men to fill them. Of course Washington could think of only one man to be the Secretary of the Treasury, and Mr. Hamilton was hardly able to contain his joy at being able to found his own currency.

"We shall base it on tens," he explained, "which will at a stroke eliminate the difficulties of converting between pounds, shillings, dollars, and all the other coins that jangle in our purses; and we shall have a national currency, so that there will be no complicated formula, as there is now, to convert the coin of New Hampshire to that of North Carolina. As the people are familiar with the name, and as it carries no memories of our oppression by the British, we shall call our coin the *dollar*, and if—"

"And these dollars," Washington interrupted—"of what size and weight will they be?"

"The weight, of course, will depend on the value we

assign to the United States dollar; as for the size, we shall consult with the men we choose to run our mint, who will be able to tell us how such and so much a weight of silver is best distributed in a coin."

"These are very important considerations from the point of view of a coin's projectile properties," said Washington. "The Spanish milled dollar travels well through the air, and possesses enough heft to carry it to its target without being too much buffeted by the wind. I should hate to see an American dollar without those properties; for men who throw dollars for sport are very particular about the dollars they throw, and might reject our United States dollar if its range and accuracy do not meet their expectations."

"I am certain you could persuade our mint to take those considerations into account," said Hamilton. "Now, as I said, multiples of ten will—"

"A milled edge also improves the grip, which for sporting purposes is one of the most important considerations."

"Yes. The grip. Now, as I was saying, we shall make our dollar divisible into tens, which we might call 'dimes,' as being, of course, the tenth part of a dollar. A tenth part of a dime would then be a 'cent,' because it is the hundredth part of—"

"I thought you said it was the tenth part."

"It is the tenth part of a dime, and therefore the hundredth part of a dollar."

"Why can't it make up its mind?"

"It is both at the same time!"

"My word! That's clever."

"And then the tenth part of a cent would be a mill, bec—"

"Because it is the millionth part of a dollar!"

"No," Hamilton explained with strained patience, "only the thousandth part."

"Then why is it called a mill?"

"Because it is—"

"Why not a thou?"

"Because the names come from Latin, or rather—"

"Oh, Latin," said Washington knowingly. "Well, Latin is another matter altogether."

Hamilton was about to say something more, but then appeared to realize that he had won as much of a victory as he was likely to win in this discussion, and resumed his earlier topic. "As I was saying, the division into tens will make calculations much easier for ordinary shopkeepers and merchants, who will find their duties lightened considerably."

"For example," said Washington, "if I buy a turkey quill at Stimson's in Alexandria for one bit, which is an eighth of a dollar, then that comes to...now let me see..."

"Twelve and a half cents," said Susanna.

"Twelve and a half? Well, that doesn't sound very easy at all. How is that easier than saying 'one bit,' Hamilton?"

"It just is!" Hamilton sputtered. "Tens are easier!"

I looked at Susanna, but she had nothing more to say. With Hamilton's explosion, she had accomplished her goal.

It is perhaps too early to speak with authority, but generations to come may remember the planting of our new capital city as the most lasting achievement of Washington's first term as President. The location of it was much debated, and it was early decided that, if the city were located on the border between two states, with perhaps land taken from both of them, it would more clearly appear to belong to the whole Union, and not to any individual state. But which border was to be chosen? To many in Congress, especially the representatives from Maryland and Pennsylvania, the border between Maryland and Pennsylvania seemed the obvious choice, as being the traditional line between North and South. Washington, however, favored a site at the head of navigation of the Potomac, which, he said, would give the new city water access to the Chesapeake, that great arm of the greater sea, and thus easy transportation to such important destinations as would not be similarly accessible from other sites. That the site was easy to reach from Mount Vernon may also have figured in his calculations. At any rate, Washington's site was chosen, because it was usually easier to give Washington what he wanted if he seemed to be set on getting it.

The business of surveying the new capital and beginning its construction gave Washington an excuse to get back to Mount Vernon, where he always felt more at home, and thus for us to get back to our house on Prince-street. Washington threw himself into the project with much enthusiasm, and he was delighted to report to us that he had found a little Frenchman named Pierre L'Enfant who was just the man to lay out his new city. He invited us to meet this man at Mount Vernon, where he would explain exactly where he had chosen to place the capital.

When we arrived at Mount Vernon, we expected to find a pale little Frenchman; but the man who was seated (on a very tall stool) at Washington's immense table, with various maps and surveys spread out before him, was nearly as dark as Susanna.

"This is Mr. Banneker, Mr. L'Enfant's assistant," Washington told us. "Mr. Banneker, my good friends Mr. Gist and Colonel Phillips."

Mr. Banneker looked puzzled for a moment; and then he appeared to recall that Washington had his quirks, and accepted the introduction as it came to him.

"And is Mr. L'Enfant here?" I asked after the usual greetings.

Mr. Banneker hesitated, but Washington answered for him: "Oh, Mr. L'Enfant is not visible in the strict sense."

Mr. Banneker smiled helplessly, but we simply accepted the information as it came to us.

"Now, Mr. Banneker," Washington continued, "what does Mr. L'Enfant think of the site?"

"Mr. L'Enfant thinks it's mostly a swamp," replied Mr. Banneker. "Mr. L'Enfant wonders why you don't put the city somewhere on higher ground."

"But this is the best possible site. Look—it's a perfect square. Where else would you find that?"

"It is a perfect square," said Banneker, "because you drew it that way on the map."

"Well, yes. Of course I did. Why would I draw it in a shape that it is not?"

Banneker paused for a moment, wearing that expression common to all who entered thus into a debate with Washington and found themselves unaccountably bested. Then he continued: "The site also includes two cities already extant, namely Georgetown and Alexandria."

"That should present no problem. They can be moved. So, since we have overcome all objections, it seems to me that Mr. L'Enfant can continue with his plans."

It happened that Mr. Banneker was staying in Alexandria on Duke-street; so, although Washington had sent a coach to fetch him, we offered to take him home in ours, an offer he gladly accepted. In the coach Susanna did not let much time pass before saying, "Tell me about Mr. L'Enfant."

Her smile left Banneker in no doubt that she understood most of the story already, so he was quite candid with us. "Mr. L'Enfant is a creation of my own. I realized, madam, that my color might obscure my abilities, and I thought if I described myself as the assistant to a well-known French engineer, I might be able to secure a better class of client. I did not expect President Washington to choose me for such an important commission, and I was certain that my deception would be discovered when he demanded to see Mr. L'Enfant personally. But when I insisted that Mr. L'Enfant could not be seen, President Washington took me more literally than I had expected. It seems there is some person by the name of Irving—"

"Not a person," I told him. "A mule."

"Ah," said Banneker, and he seemed not to know what to say after that.

"I don't believe the deception was necessary," said Susanna. "The President believes I am a white man named Phillips. That the fact is otherwise should, in spite of my masculine garb, be apparent to you."

"Abundantly," said Banneker, with an expression that brought me a momentary pang of jealousy. "That said, will you betray me to him? I have no doubt I deserve it, but—"

"I do not think it would be possible to change Washington's mind about you," I said. "He has known my wife Susanna for thirteen years, and not even the arrival of our children could persuade him that she is anything other than Colonel Phillips." I own I added these details partly in order to forestall any false impressions Banneker might have about Susanna. When a man possesses a single precious jewel, he may at times seem overcautious.

"So you will not betray me?"

"Vive L'Enfant, as far as I'm concerned."

Banneker soon had a draft of his plan ready, and Susanna and I, along with Parson Weems, were privileged to be at Mount Vernon when he presented it to Washington.

"You see that the pattern of the streets is very rational," Banneker explained. "They go north and south, or east and west; the former numbered, the latter named by letters of the alphabet."

"Oh, yes, this is very fine," said Washington. "I foresee a mighty city rising here—a city whose position at the head of navigation on the Potomac will give rise to undreamt-of prosperity; a city of globe-circling commerce, of gleaming towers and verdant parks; a center of learning and the arts—"

"A city called Washington?" asked Parson Weems.

"No, of course not. Don't be absurd. It would be presumptuous of me in the extreme to establish a capital bearing my own name. I was thinking of 'Columbia,' after the great navigator who discovered the New World. How does that sound?"

"A fine name," Susanna said with what sounded like relief.

"Now, this round thing here," Washington continued—"what is that?"

"A natural basin, which we shall improve as a promenade for the residents. I was thinking it might look especially splendid in the spring if we planted the perimeter with cherry trees."

"I think not," said Washington, suddenly stiff.

"But the blossoms would make—"

"No cherries. I particularly desire you, for very good and sufficient reasons, not to plant cherry trees."

"Of course if you insist—"

"I think we can do without the cherries.—Now, you have all these streets going straight up and down or back and forth."

"Yes, sir."

"And this is the President's house here. And the Capitol, where the Congress meets, here. Now, what happens if the President needs to go to the Capitol to address Congress?"

"Then he can walk down past this street, and this, and then turn left and walk straight to the Capitol like this," replied Banneker.

"Would it not," asked Washington, picking up the quill and dipping it in the ink, "be more efficient to have a street connecting the two points directly?" He drew a straight line between the President's house and the Capitol on the map.

Banneker looked horrified. "But it destroys the logical symmetry of it all. If you—"

"And then to get from here to here you could have a street going directly like this." He drew a diagonal straight across Mr. Banneker's neat horizontals and verticals. "And from here to here" (he drew another line), "and here to here, and here to here."

"But I had a perfectly neat system of numbered and lettered streets!" And then, recollecting himself, Banneker added, "I mean, Mr. L'Enfant had."

"I'm sure Mr. L'Enfant will see the wisdom of these improvements. We could name these more direct streets after states of the Union. This one could be Pennsylvania, this one New-York, this one Virginia, this one Wisconsin, this one Georgia, and so on."

"There's no state called 'Wisconsin.'"

"We could make one to match the street. Plenty of room in the Northwest. I don't see why some of my land can't be set aside for states with whimsical names."

Mr. Banneker sighed and said, "I'll present the idea to Mr. L'Enfant."

Later, as we were on our way home in our coach, Susanna asked me, "Will anyone be able to find his way in our capital city once Washington has done with altering the plans?"

"Probably not," I replied. "But consider the advantages. If we ever go to war again, the enemy will never successfully invade our capital. Any invading force would find itself hopelessly lost and easily overcome."

"I do love your good cheer," said Susanna, "but please, just this once, will you admit to me that the man is an imbecile?"

Chapter XIV.

Washington campaigns for a second term.—Whiskey Rebellion.—Hamilton's strategy against the rebels.—Susanna suggests Washington take command.—Brackenridge's wit, and its destructive effects.—Treaty scandal.—Washington retires.—His farewell address.

Toward the end of his third year as President, Washington began to consider the question of who should occupy the office for the next term.

"I am, of course" (he said), "exceedingly reluctant to take a second term, for the exigencies of the office weigh heavily upon me. The business of being surrounded by lackeys who tend to one's every whim, and of being treated with universal respect, and of having to drink the very best Madeira every evening in the very best company, must eventually be wearing to a simple republican farmer. Nevertheless, if my country were to call me to a second term in office, my conscience would forbid me from making light of my country's demands. No, I should be forced to answer the call, even at the cost of another four years of luxury and universal adulation. It will be cloying, but if it has to be done, I am not one to shirk my duty. You, Weems" (for we were dining with Parson Weems, on one of Washington's rare evenings away from his onerous duties), "may let my sentiments be known in some inconspicuous way, for I would not force myself upon the people."

But of course Hamilton was restrained by no considerations of inconspicuousness, and he took on the management of Washington's campaign with his accustomed vigor. The result, as readers will recall, was that the people overwhelmingly returned electors for Washington, and his presidency continued for another four years. These years, however, were marked by more difficulties than Washington had expected to meet, and he was forced to confront, on occasion, the unaccustomed sensation of not being universally loved.

One of the most severe tests of his resolve was the Whiskey Rebellion, which enraged Hamilton to such a degree that I thought the man might succumb to apoplexy. A tax having been placed on ardent spirits, certain men in the western part of Pennsylvania, where rye whiskey was the staple food, refused to submit to the collection of it, and had even attacked some of the gentlemen charged with the collecting. Hamilton persuaded Washington to put him in command of a body of soldiers to be sent across the mountains to crush the rebellion, and the enthusiasm with which he planned his campaign was startling to see.

"Of course they must be crushed utterly," Hamilton said as he explained his plan to Susanna and me. "My strategy will be to come upon them with overwhelming force, thus teaching them that the United States Tax Code is not to be trifled with. I shall besiege and take Pittsburgh, burn the city to ashes, slaughter all the male inhabitants, and distribute the females as prizes to the soldiers. Once we have made an example of the largest settlement in those parts, the terror thus inspired will doubtless induce the rebels to submit forthwith, after which they can be sold as slaves to the islands in the Caribbean. Thus we shall establish the principle that the rule of law prevails in these United States."

Susanna said nothing, and I was mildly surprised when Hamilton left the room without a blackened eye. But the next day, when we were with Washington, Susanna made a suggestion that ultimately had the effect of changing the aspect of the expedition considerably.

"Do you not think, sir, that as commander in chief of the army, you have a duty to take charge of this expedition yourself?"

"A duty? I had not thought of it, but..."

"The United States need their greatest military mind at this time of crisis," said Susanna. "It is time for President Washington to don the buff and blue and become General Washington once more."

"My word, Phillips, you're right! I must see my tailor."

Hamilton was furious at this change of plans, but of course he could say nothing against it. Washington visited his tailor—he now measured just under seventeen feet tall—and as soon as his new uniform was ready, we set out (for he insisted on having Susanna and me with him) to cross the Alleghenies.

Civilization had made great progress since our expeditions against the French many years before. At the flourishing town of Bedford in Pennsylvania, we met up with Hugh Henry Brackenridge, a prominent judge and literary man of Pittsburgh, who had come to meet Washington along the way in the hope of working out some peaceful resolution to the crisis. This Judge Brackenridge was a man famous for his wit, whose very amusing books had reached me in Alexandria, and I was glad of the opportunity to make his personal acquaintance.

We put up for the evening in a newly built inn west of Bedford, whose ample interior was just large enough to accommodate Washington if he stooped when he stood. Susanna and I having been distracted in our chamber, we arrived late to dinner, and came in just in time to hear Brackenridge finishing one of his amusing stories.

"And I replied, 'I know what you mean very well; you want to have a shot at me, but I have no inclination to hit you, and I am afraid you would hit me; I pray thee therefore have me excused.' "

I had heard only the end of the story, but it must have been very clever, as the rest of the company were laughing boisterously—all, that is, except for Washington, who sat impassive, looking indeed very dignified, but not even smiling. I saw that Brackenridge was watching Washington's reaction, and I could see in Brackenridge's countenance the determination to make the great man laugh; his pride was hurt, and he was going to try harder. I ought to have taken him aside on some pretext and explained to him the peculiar nature of Washington's sense of humor, but these things, alas! are clear in hindsight alone.

"Which reminds me," Brackenridge continued, "of the story of the Indian-treaty man and his king of the Kickapoos"; and thus began a very amusing anecdote which had the whole company helpless with laughter —all, of course, but Washington, whose expression of serene benevolence did not change in the least.

That failure spurred Brackenridge to even greater efforts, and tears were running down the cheeks of most of the guests by the time he had finished with his tale of a hard-fought election in the west country of Pennsylvania. But Washington was not moved, and Brackenridge would not accept failure, until at last he had worn himself out and us as well. Washington thanked him for his very informative discourse, and I think Brackenridge was near ready to bite his own tongue off in frustration.

The long table was cleared and then made up to serve as Washington's bed; Susanna and I went upstairs to our own chamber, extinguished the light, and never once considered the dreadful danger that awaited us,

Some time after midnight I was awakened by a thunderous crash that shook the bed. It had been more than ten years since Yorktown, but my first thought was that a cannon had gone off quite nearby. Then I heard whooping and pounding, and I knew that the long fuse ignited by Brackenridge earlier had at last reached the keg. Washington was laughing, and the sheer number of Brackenridge's anecdotes, jokes, and aphorisms had led to an explosion of titanic proportions.

Susanna was already out of bed and had managed to light a candle in what was left of the fire. Another loud crash, and the whole floor shook, and then more whoops and howls, and a series of rapid hammerings that caused the whole inn to quake.

"Can you do anything?" Susanna asked me as she pulled on a robe.

"You know as well as I do that nothing can stop him once the fit is upon him."

Suddenly the house shook in a very alarming way. Washington was whooping and laughing, and now shouts from elsewhere in the inn had joined the appalling din.

"I wonder whether we ought—" Susanna began, but she was interrupted by an extended crashing and smashing sound, as if a whole china cupboard had fallen over.

"You go see whether you can stop him, or get him outside," Susanna told me. "I'll go get—"

There was another cataclysmic crash, and the ominous sound of creaking and splintering wood.

"Go!" Susanna shouted. "I'll get the rest out!"

I dashed out into the hall, where I found the other guests, or at least a good many of them, up and in an advanced state of panic. Another crash rocked the house, and toppled several of the guests in the hall; and when we regained our footing, the floor was on a pronounced bias. Susanna was urging the rest down the stairs; I seized a candle from one of them and ran down ahead of the group. As I reached the bottom of the stairway, a huge beam fell in the front parlor, sending plaster dust billowing though the whole ground floor. The pounding and crashing and whooping continued as I dashed back to the end of the hall and into the great dining-room, which looked like Lisbon after the earthquake. The table had fallen to the floor, most of the chairs were piles of splinters, and a great cabinet filled with china and glassware lay in a field of shards of all colors. There were holes in the walls, and the outer wall looked dangerously skewed.

And Washington was still howling, kicking, and pounding. "Ten dollars for your scalp!" he bellowed, and then fell over so that his head crashed through the wall into the front parlor, his feet meanwhile kicking holes in the planks of the floor.

"Washington!" I shouted. "Come out before the house comes down!"

"They tarred and feathered the *turkey!*" he howled, rolling over and taking a good bit of the wall with him. This was too much for the floor above, which began to sag with an appalling ripping and cracking sound.

"Washington! Washington, the ceiling is collapsing!"

But Washington was still in the grip of his fit. Years earlier I might have dragged him out, but he had long since passed the dimensions where that was possible.

Suddenly a beam came down, and another beside it, just missing both of us and lying diagonally with one end of each on the floor and the other above us supported by the outside wall. And I do verily believe those beams saved both our lives, for now the whole house was coming down around us. It was the closest I have ever come to Armageddon, and it seemed to go on for hours, though I suppose it must have been less than a minute. Only the fallen beams above us, and the fragment of floor they supported, kept us from being crushed. It was only a temporary reprieve, however; for now the pile of rubble that once was an inn had caught fire, and we were trapped. I tried shouting, but I could not make myself heard over the din of Washington's laughter. Fortunately he was still pounding and kicking, and the rubble in his pedal regions was flying in all directions. But for some bruises and cuts, I was not injured, and I was able to add my efforts to clear a passage, which were augmented by the efforts of the escaped guests outside; and before the flames could reach us, we were safely out of the wreckage, with Susanna clinging to me and kissing my scratches, and Washington now reduced to helpless sniggering. We were without shelter, but the burning inn sufficed to keep us warm.

The next morning there was nothing left of the inn but two stone chimneys and some fragments of charred wood clinging to them. But Washington made sure to attach one of his brass plaques to the remains. It is still in place today, so that if, on the road west of Bedford, you stop to examine the picturesque ruin now slowly being reclaimed by the devouring woods, you may learn that once upon a time George Washington slept there.

The end of the Whiskey Rebellion was something of an anticlimax. Washington, who enjoyed the trappings of war but preferred wars in which no one was seriously hurt, summoned the leaders of the rebellion to a parley. They came prepared to defy him, but they did not come prepared for his size. The appearance of a seventeen-foot Washington at the parley routed all opposition. Washington pardoned everyone, heard their grievances, and promised to ask Congress to consider them; but meanwhile he desired them to give him no reason to come back with an even more overwhelming force. They assured him that they had no desire to see him there again, and thus the matter was ended.

It might have been a happier time for Washington

if all the crises of his administration had been so easily resolved. Partisan strife, however, began to creep into our government, and some in Congress were looking for excuses to oppose President Washington. They found one in the secret treaty negotiated by the mysterious John J., who always refused to reveal his surname even to his most intimate acquaintances, and responded to every attempt at guessing the name with an enigmatic smile. This treaty granted certain concessions to the British, and congressmen were not uniformly happy with all its provisions, raising questions especially about the clause granting any British ship the right to make rude gestures at any American ship without reprisals in kind. The Congress demanded to see the notes and memoranda generated by the President and his associates on the subject of the treaty. Washington quite correctly replied that there were no notes or memoranda: when he thought something ought to be done, he did it.

But then, somehow, the fact of Mr. Shelton's secret recordings came to light—I have always suspected that Hamilton had something to do with it, but I have no proof—and Congress began to demand the president's secret "tapes." These Washington steadfastly refused to turn over, saying that it was the privilege of the executive to keep his private deliberations secret. Eventually, however, he agreed to have the relevant tapes transcribed (for he would not lose his originals). This course of action quelled the complaints for a time until it was found that, in one of the transcriptions which most interested the men in Congress, there was a gap of eighteen and a half pages, and that Mr. Shelton could not account for how he had lost the corresponding section of "tape."

Thus the latter part of Washington's presidency was filled with wrangling and vituperation, neither of which came naturally to the great man. And that is why, though it surprised the country and the world, Washington's decision not to seek a third term did not surprise me.

"Hamilton," he told Susanna and me, "has drafted an address for me, in which I shall announce my decision and offer a few parting words of wisdom to the people of my country. It will be good to have done with this business."

At the mention of Hamilton's name, Susanna's ears seemed to move forward. "I should very much like to see this address," she said, and Washington was happy to oblige her. Having read a few lines, she told him, "If you would like, I could give this a thorough perusal and correct a few trifling errors which have crept into the text, doubtless owing to the haste of the composition."

"Oh, yes, Phillips, that would be very kind of you," Washington replied; and so we ended by taking Mr. Hamilton's manuscript home with us, where Susanna sat down and began running long lines through whole paragraphs of text.

"What are you doing?" I asked her.

"I am making a few trifling corrections," she replied. "For example, here, where it says, 'You must destroy their name from under heaven; you must put every male to the sword; you must leave nothing that breathes alive'—I am correcting it so that it does not say that."

"I suppose Hamilton's text admits of some improvement," I said.

"I have also removed some specific references to Mr. Jefferson in which his parentage is called into question."

"Probably a prudent alteration."

"And the section that compares Mr. Adams to the back end of certain domestic animals has been struck out as well."

"I'm sure Washington will be grateful to you for your diligence."

And so Washington's farewell address appeared in a somewhat milder form than that in which Hamilton had prepared it, but it was generally well received all the same. When he delivered it in public, however, Washington added one paragraph of his own which did not generally appear in the published versions of the address, and so I reproduce it here:

"It is also essential that you resist to the utmost degree the baneful influence of certain members of the animal kingdom, who, though they may not be visible in the strict sense, are, you may be sure, working incessantly to undermine the system of government, and the individual liberties, which we have labored so assiduously to obtain, and which are the most precious inheritance of our children. In warning you against the machinations of malevolent invisible animals, I am certain I give you no new information; but it is my hope that my words may remain in your memory, perhaps to recur to your minds at a time when their influence will be most profitable."

The night before he turned over the presidency to Mr. Adams, Washington had a supper with a few of his most intimate friends; and, after the rest had gone, he desired that Susanna and I remain a while longer. Having poured us each another glass of Madeira, he told us, "I shall, of course, be retiring to Mount Vernon; and it would please me very much if I could have the assistance of both of you in maintaining the estate, which I intend to run as a model of a plantation managed on rational principles. I plan to leave some of it forested for game, and I believe you, Gist, would be the very man to take care of that; and I thought I could put Phillips in charge of the slaves. I hope I am not asking too much of you, but the fact is that it would cheer me greatly to see two of my oldest friends often on the grounds, and—Gist, do you think Phillips needs a thump on the back? He seems to be choking on his Madeira."

CHAPTER XV.

*Washington's retirement.—Susanna manages the slaves.—
Washington discovers the meaning of slavery,—Equestrian accident.—Illness and medical treatment.—Washington's last advice.—Death, burial, and tributes.—
Birth of G. W. Gist.—Parson Weems' book.*

WASHINGTON soon settled into a comfortable routine at
Mount Vernon. He experimented with crop rotation,
investing in a large turntable for the purpose, which
was driven by oxen and could rotate a quarter-acre of
crops as many as three times in an hour if the oxen
were sufficiently motivated. He also expressed a desire
to resume equestrian exercises, which presented some
difficulty, as horses tended to shy away from a man
who was nineteen feet two inches tall, and probably
there was not a horse bred of sufficient size to bear
Washington comfortably in his current dimensions.
Our old friend Mr. Banneker, however, knew of a
clever young engineer by the name of Fulton who
was, he said, doing marvelous things with steam
power. With the help of one of our better sculptors,
Mr. Fulton created a steam-powered horse that, provided we kept to the smooth drives we laid down all
over the estate, served very well, though it required
half an hour to make enough steam for locomotion,
and was subject to occasional mechanical failures. After a few frightening accidents, Mr. Fulton rigged a

mechanism by which the steam-horse rolled to a stop whenever Washington fell off, which diminished our worries considerably.

Susanna and I divided out time between our town-house in Alexandria and Mount Vernon, where Washington treated Crispus and Jane almost as if they were his own children, and Mrs. Washington was ever finding excuses to stuff them with pies. I never was certain where Washington thought our children had come from, nor was I sure that he understood the mechanism by which children are introduced into the world; but children never had a better friend than the General.

Susanna's management of the slaves took the form of making them very comfortable and expecting little in the way of work from them; but even though Washington now had the only estate in Virginia where the slave quarters were more opulent than the main house, with a large library, a lecture hall, a ballroom, an orangery, and a number of other conveniences;— in spite of these things, I say, Susanna was not happy, nor did she believe the slaves were happy so long as they lacked that liberty for which no physical comfort could compensate.

One evening, about two years after he had left the presidency, Washington asked her (over the Madeira, as usual), "How are the slaves, Phillips? Are they happy?"

He had not phrased the question in that way before, but now that he had done so, Susanna did not withhold her opinion.

"I do not believe they are, General, and in their present condition I do not believe there is anything that could make them happy."

"But why is that, Phillips?" Washington asked. "Have we neglected anything they need?"

"We have neglected nothing that could tend to their physical comfort, but I still believe that they can never be happy in a condition of servitude."

"Well, I must say, it sounds like rank ingratitude to me, but I suppose if they don't like working for me they can go somewhere else and do whatever appeals to them."

Susanna looked confused. "No they can't."

"Why not?"

"Because they're property!"

"Property!" Washington sputtered. "Of course not! They're human beings. How can they be property?"

"But, good heavens, General, what did you think 'slaves' meant?"

"I thought it meant they came from eastern Europe."

"It means they're property! You own them. That's what the law says. You can do anything with them, and they can do nothing about it. They have no rights, no liberties, no lives of their own. That is what it means to be slaves."

Washington turned to me. "Gist, is this true?"

"Yes, Washington," I replied.

"But this is monstrous! Why was I not told of this?"

"We presumed you knew," said Susanna.

"But all men are created equal! How can some be the property of others? No, by heaven, I won't be long in doing something about this! Virginia is a civilized country; we shall have no relics of barbarism here! Phillips, after the levee tomorrow, you will help me make alternate arrangements for Mount Vernon, and then, upon my word! we shall work until not a slave is left in Virginia!"

He stormed off, more angry than I had ever seen him.

Susanna gaped after him, and then closed her jaw and looked thoughtful for a moment.

"He really is an imbecile," she said. "And right now I am very glad of it."

We were staying at Mount Vernon that night, in preparation for the levee the next morning; and after Susanna and the children had gone to bed, Washington and I stayed up quite late talking—or, rather, Washington talked, and I listened. I think he was quite upset by his discovery of slavery, but there was more to his discontent than that.

"I feel the effects of age, Gist," said he, "more than I have done in the past; there were things I thought I would accomplish in my youth, and now I see that I shall never accomplish them."

"You have quite some time to work on them," I said with a smile.

"It is not so much that I cannot do them," Washington replied; "it is that the things I would have done are no longer worth doing. Once we were young, and the world was vast enough to hold our imaginations and our ambitions; now we are grown old, and how diminished everything is! The men we call great are as tiny puppets to the men of old days; our cities grow, and yet they no longer fill our hearts with a lively sense of boundless possibilities; our country extends its borders, and yet it is a little thing on a little earth, no longer the vast unknown clinging to the edge of the illimitable unknowable. This very house, Gist, was a grand palace when my brother built it; I have extended it, yet it has grown small and familiar. Ah, Gist, I now understand the tales of primordial giants: for in the youth of the world all accomplishments must have been magnificent; but men have multiplied, and their deeds have filled the earth. When we are young, we are filled with the passionate longing to conquer the unconquerable world. As we grow old, we find that we have conquered it, and there are no more worlds to conquer. This is the tragedy of every man's life. The world is small, Gist! The world is small, and filled with little men, and I am so weary of looking down on it!"

The next morning was the monthly levee at Mount Vernon, where Washington made himself available to all and sundry. We had built stands near the river where Washington's guests could sit and see Washington at eye level as he rode past on his steam-horse, stopping to speak to his visitors without stooping.

We managed to get Washington mounted on the horse without incident, and the mechanism seemed to be working flawlessly. It was a bitterly cold morning, and snow was in the air; but that had not prevented a few hundred visitors from coming out to pay their respects to the great man.

These occasions were always happy ones for the General, and he took his time riding down the stands, stopping every few feet to speak to someone in the crowd, to bless a child, to thank an old veteran. About two-thirds of the way down the row he stopped in front of a family with a young child, perhaps a year old, and greeted the smiling parents.

"His name is Washington," the proud mother told him, holding up the indifferent and unimpressed little boy. "We named him for you."

"A compliment I shall treasure to the end of my life," Washington graciously replied. "And what is his family name?"

The mother answered, "Irving."

"Irving!" Washington jumped back in his saddle, the natural consequence of which was that he fell off the horse and into the icy waters of the Potomac. He splashed about in a very undignified way, while women screamed and several of us ran to offer our assistance. But he pulled himself out of the water and insisted on remounting the horse; then he continued the levee until everyone who wanted to speak with him had a chance to do so. He would not go in and change his wet clothes until he had seen off his last visitor.

We were not surprised, therefore, that he spent the rest of the day in bed, and that he woke up the next morning with a sore throat that nearly deprived him of his voice. Washington himself was of the opinion that it was not a serious indisposition, but Mrs. Washington insisted on calling in a physician. I myself rode out to fetch the physician Mrs. Washington trusted most; and there are times when I wish I had fallen into a ditch and broken my neck before I reached his house in Alexandria.

Dr. Polk lived in a very fine house on Duke-street. When he heard that General Washington was ill, he could hardly disguise his satisfaction at the large fee that would doubtless be his no matter what the results of his ministrations. He was a little round man with a big round face, which somehow grew broader without actually erupting into a smile when he heard my news. He told me he would be ready directly; then he trotted upstairs, and a quarter-hour later trotted down with a large case under each arm. He had already summoned his driver, for a coach awaited him in front of the house—a coach and four, suggesting that his practice was a successful one. I allowed myself to be reassured by that observation.

When we arrived at Mount Vernon, I immediately brought Dr. Polk into Washington's chamber on the ground floor, the only part of the house where the rooms were large enough to accommodate him as long as he did not stand fully upright. As we made the long march from the General's feet to his head, Dr. Polk explained to me that he intended to stay for several days, as in such cases as these it was critical for the patient to be bled frequently until the crisis had passed.

"Bled?" I asked, and I am certain that my voice betrayed my alarm.

"When the humors have become unbalanced," said Dr. Polk, "it is essential to restore the proper balance. An excess of the sanguine humor is the most common cause of such illnesses as these, and fortunately the most easily corrected."

We had now reached the region of the head, where Mrs. Washington was sitting, and Dr. Polk explained to her and the General what he had just finished explaining to me. "All I need," he said, "is a large tub or vat, or possibly a barrel, and we may begin at once."

Mrs. Washington was not long in having a large

wine-vat, cut in half, brought into the room, and Dr. Polk proceeded at once to the business of disposing of Washington's excess sanguinary fluid. The vat had already made three trips out to be dumped in the garden by the time evening came; then Dr. Polk closed off the tap, with the promise of more bleeding on the morrow.

The next day, Washington was paler and weaker, which Dr. Polk took as a sign that more bleeding was needed. Prodigious quantities of blood went out into the garden, but in spite of all the bleeding, Washington only grew weaker. Susanna asked more than once whether the General might not need some of that blood, but Dr. Polk explained that it was common for the patient to weaken temporarily in treating cases of humoral imbalance, but recovery would follow provided an aggressive course of treatment was pursued to its conclusion.

Washington only grew weaker, however, and on the third day Dr. Polk tried blistering in addition to the bleeding. On the fourth day he added a bit of cautery to the regimen, but in spite of these treatments Washington did not improve.

The signs, in fact, were worrying. Washington dictated a new will, and began to speak, when he could speak, as one who expected to be taken from the world soon. Parson Weems had been summoned, and Susanna and I sat in the great chamber where the great man—he was now twenty feet and an inch tall —lay stretched out on the bed that had been constructed for him, with Mrs. Washington in constant attendance.

"Please take no more trouble about me," Washington said, "and especially tell Dr. Polk that I shall not be requiring his services any longer. It may be hard to die, but I am not afraid to go. However—Martha, my dearest, and my dear friend Parson Weems, if you could leave me for just a few moments, I have something to say in private to Gist and Phillips."

Mrs. Washington kissed his vast forehead, and she and the Parson walked silently out of the room, closing the door soundlessly behind them.

Susanna and I were now alone with the great man, whose breathing grew more and more labored, and his voice more hoarse; but it was clear that he had something to say that was worth any labor to him. We stood next to his head and listened attentively.

"Gist, Phillips, I have left some things unsaid to this day, because I believed that no good could come of saying them, or at least that the harm done would exceed the benefit. As a result, I have the impression that you especially, Phillips, take me for a fool.—No, do not contradict me; it may or may not be so; I say only that I have that impression, and it is because I have not said what I know about you, wherefore I suppose you must have imagined that I did not know it."

Susanna laid a gentle hand on his shoulder, but did not venture to speak. Washington coughed a few times halfheartedly, as if he knew he was expected to cough but had really lost interest in coughing. Then he spoke again:

"I have known for many years that you and Gist share—share a love after the Grecian manner. No one who knows you both as well as I know you could possibly miss it. I do not condemn you. I am a broad-minded man of the world, and I know that in classical times love between men was looked on with indulgence, and often indeed praised as superior to the love between men and women. But these are not classical times. I say not that you must end your love: I am not such a fool as to believe you would do so, even if I adjured you to it as my dying wish. I merely urge you to greater discretion. While I lived, no one would speak against you for fear of offending me. When I am gone, you will not have that protection. Already dark clouds of partisan strife are on the horizon. Jefferson— But I will not speak of politics, except to warn you both that in me you lose a friend who sincerely desired nothing but your good, and where you will find another such I know not. And now, my beloved friends, if I must leave you, farewell. I should like to see Martha again."

We left the General with heavy hearts, and sent Mrs. Washington back in to him; and then all we could do was sit in the hall and wait.

"There was never a greater fool born on earth," said Susanna, squeezing my hand. I turned to see her cheek wet with running tears.

It was about a quarter-hour later that Susanna and I both heard a strange and startling sound, something very like the braying of a mule. It was so close that it seemed to be right outside the window; but when we stood to investigate, we could see nothing there. We sat back down, neither of us daring to speak.

Shortly afterward, Mrs. Washington emerged to tell us, with remarkable composure, that General Washington was no more.

Susanna suddenly stood and rushed out of the hall

into the great drawing-room. I spoke a few words of consolation to Mrs. Washington, and then turned to follow Susanna. I could already hear her shouting.

"You killed him!"

She had found Dr. Polk in the drawing-room with Parson Weems, and she had turned the full force of an uncharacteristic fury on the doctor.

"You tortured him like a Spanish inquisitor, and then you killed the only great man we had!"

Dr. Polk was already standing. "Madam, I am very sorry for your grief, but—"

"He could have survived anything except you! You killed him, you murdering bastard!"

Dr. Polk was of course sympathetic, but he would not let her accusations pass without defending himself. "The General had everything the Hippocratic art could provide him. Nothing was omitted that could have served to balance the humors and render—"

He had not expected the blow from Susanna's fist, which connected with his skull so forcefully that the doctor fell flat on the floor, where he remained immobile while Susanna ran out of the room and up the stairs.

"Could you tend to him, please?" I asked Parson Weems. I followed Susanna upstairs to console her. But for the moment she was inconsolable, and all I could do was join her in weeping.

The news of Washington's death plunged his country into deep mourning. Even across the sea, when the news reached Europe, the British and French both fired twenty guns in his honor, successfully killing twelve British and fourteen French sailors. The great man's earthly remains were laid to rest on his own beloved estate, and the grave was covered with the largest ledger yet carved in America, on which was inscribed, in neat Roman capitals, the simple message,

GEORGE WASHINGTON SLEPT HERE.

By the provisions of his will, all of Washington's slaves were emancipated with generous legacies. Some stayed to work as tour guides, for Mount Vernon quickly became a site of patriotic pilgrimage; but many went to work for Mr. Banneker. With Washington gone, it was no longer possible to maintain the fiction of the talented little Frenchman; so with Susanna's help a story was concocted to the effect that the irascible little man had stomped off in high dudgeon, but Mr. Banneker had fortunately been able to reconstruct the plans of the city from memory. This supposed feat added markedly to his reputation, and thus to his business, and the firm prospered.

About two months after Washington's death, Susanna, who was now forty-three years old, surprised me with the news that she was expecting another child. When, seven months later, our new son was born, Susanna insisted that only one name could possibly be appropriate; and so the infant was christened George Washington Gist. Thus, in a sense, the story of George Washington ends, not with a death, but with a birth.

Almost exactly a year after Washington's death, I had dinner with Parson Weems. He had come to Alexandria to arrange for the printing of his new tract, "On the Detection of Papists by the Olfactory

Sense," and our coming together so close to the scene of our happiest days naturally conduced to an evening spent reminiscing about our departed friend. It was a pastime we were all the more willing to indulge in as being almost the only two men who had followed Washington in all his adventures, from the beginning of the French and Indian War to his last fatal accident. Susanna (who had never thought much of Parson Weems) had retired with little George, and a pleasant melancholy suffused the atmosphere of my front parlor as we talked late into the night; until Parson Weems made a statement that, though no fault of his own, unsettled me.

"In fact," he said, "I intend to write a biography of our friend Washington."

I own that this news hit me with unexpected force. I had nearly completed this memoir, and now Parson Weems was preparing a book on exactly the same subject! Still, I could hardly blame him for that.

"I suppose no one is better qualified to write it," I said mildly. "You and I are perhaps the only two men in the world who have first-hand knowledge of Washington's entire career, from the beginning to the very end. You, as a literary man, are obviously the best qualified to give the public the truth about our friend."

"Oh, I don't think the truth is what the public wants at all," said Weems.

"What do you mean by that?"

"Great as the man was, the American people have made him greater," he explained. "They have made him the embodiment of all the virtues they admire, and they attribute their success as a newborn among the nations entirely to his almost-divine agency. He is their Moses, their Solon, their Confucius. They have elevated him to the pantheon; they have placed him among the stars so that they may look up to him forevermore. And they are right to do so. They don't need Washington the man; they need Washington the guiding principle. As long as they can look up to him and see everything that is best in themselves, they will be inspired to outdo one another in virtue, and these United States of America will grow and flourish and draw all men to themselves. No, the truth about Washington is the last thing the public needs. I shall give the young people of America, not the Washington that was, but the Washington that ought to have been."

I thought his argument was a good one, and at the same time I felt a strong sense of relief. We might have chosen the same subject, but we were not writing the same book. Parson Weems has his Washington, and I have mine. He has given America and the world the man they imagined, the Washington they wish to remember. I have given you the Washington I knew; and I am not ashamed to say that, imperfect though he may have been, I loved the man as he was.

A Brief Afterword, Written in the Year 2020.

This *Memoir*, though in its day it was much read, never had the success of Weems' *Life of George Washington*, and by the time of the Civil War it had been largely forgotten. When it was decided to investigate the unusual phenomena at Washington's tomb, however, this book seemed to be the only one that offered any clues that might eventually point to a solution of the mystery. Since copies of the original are now scarce and expensive, it was thought that making it available in this economical form might encourage further research.

The grave of Washington was measured many times in the nineteenth century, and the measurements vary by no more than an inch. In all cases, they document a ledger, inscribed with the simple epitaph GEORGE WASHINGTON SLEPT HERE, that was approximately twenty-five feet long. The earliest photographs of the tomb confirm the measurements, at least as well as we can judge by comparing the ledger with other objects in the tomb.

Some time after the First World War, however, visitors to Mount Vernon began to notice that the ledger did not seem to be quite as big as the guide books said it ought to be. By the 1950s, the shrinking had attracted the attention of a few researchers, but the Mount Vernon Ladies' Association was reluctant to allow any examination for fear of damaging the precious relics. The shrinking accelerated in the late twentieth century, however, and by the twenty-first it was so rapid that the Ladies' Association finally decided to allow a scientific and archaeological investigation, in the hope of stabilizing the structure.

The investigators could not find anything to account for the shrinking. They could only report that the grave was covered by a ledger that appeared to be made of native stone with no unusual properties; that there was nothing to indicate that the stone had been replaced; and that the tomb, when opened, proved to contain the skeletal remains of a male approximately four feet nine inches in height.